2ND CHANCES

JULIE PICKENS

For all who believe that God can give

Second Chances

Table of Contents

This page was left blank intentionally.

Acknowledgements

Thanks be to God for giving me the gift of imagination and the perseverance it took to finish this project.

Second, a huge thank you to the people He placed in my life who were instrumental in my writing this book. My mother-in-law Annie Lee Pickens, who was my biggest cheerleader. I miss her daily. My husband W.V. Pickens 111, who supported me through the whole process. My children, Lyric Ann Pickens and Julian Gerrard Pickens, who believed in my ability to write even before I did.

Third, thank you to my Chicago Bar Association family. Larry Kay who in the beginning taught me the basic principles of writing. Maia Campbell, Erika Griffin, Swanella Brooks, Juanita and Richard Aldana all of whom encouraged me to go for it. I couldn't have done it without them pushing me. Terrence Murphy, Executive Director of The Chicago Bar Association, made me feel so proud when he told me, he would buy a copy of my book when it was finished. I don't think he knew how he blessed me by saying that. Thank you, to all the other friends and family who I did not mention by name because the list is so long.

Last but not least, I'd like to thank my Greater Mt Calvary MBC family. They have shown me nothing but love and support in everything I do. God Bless you all.

This page was left blank intentionally.

Forward

I have known my wife Julie for almost 40 years. We've been married for 34 of those 40 years and have 2 wonderful children Lyric and Julian. I too am a receiver of a Second Chance from God. Julie is my second wife. I've watched her grow from a young, shy, full of hopes and dreams woman, to a strong, mature, full of life woman of God. To know her is to love her. She can light up any room. Her wittiness, her beauty, and her poise makes her the perfect First Lady for me. Julie has been blessed with many gifts but, I believe her writing gift will be a blessing to many. Keep up the good work.

Pastor W.V. Pickens 111

Greater Mt. Calvary Baptist Church

Indianapolis, Indiana

This page was left blank intentionally.

Chapter 1

Rose laid in the darkness of her cell remembering oh too well how she got there. She kept repeating to herself, 7 years, 7 years, 2,555 days locked up in this place. On the 2,556th day, Morton Dunn will die. I'll kill him slowly she thought, just like he killed my grandmother.

Rose's hatred for Morton Dunn was the only thing that kept her sane. Many of the girls in lockup lost their minds not being able to cope, but not Rose. Hatred drove her. Rose made it no secret how she felt about M.D., that's what he called himself when she and her grandma met him.

Bea took a liking to Rose right away when she saw her come down the corridor, proud as if she was a Nubian Princess. The new girls on the block always got the usual fanfare, kisses thrown at them, yells of whose woman they would be, or even spat on. It didn't seem to faze Rose.

The guards brought her to Bea's cell. Rose walked right in pass Bea as if she wasn't there. Bea tried to be as cordial as possible. She introduced herself.

"Hi! I'm Bea, as in bumble," Bea giggled at her pun, Rose did not. Bea thought to herself, this one is going to be hard to soften up.

Bea tried again, this time using a different approach, "uh, welcome to my humble abode."

Rose, looked at Bea long and hard then said without blinking, "don't bother, Bea is it? I'm not here to make any friends. I'm here to do my time and that's it. Now if you don't mind leave me alone."

Bea responded with a bit of her own sarcasm. "Honey, there is plenty of alone in this place, but take my advice, if you know what's good for you, you won't stay alone too long."

It wasn't long before Rose warmed up to Bea. She got tired of the other women bothering her. They knew if she was a friend of Bea's not to mess with her. Bea had made her own reputation already serving 20 years of a life sentence. Every chance Rose got she would watch Bea as if she were studying her. She'd look away each time Bea caught her looking.

Finally, Bea decided not to ignore her stares. "Rose, is there something on your mind?"

Rose hesitated at first then blurted out. "I'm just curious that's all. I've only heard bits and pieces of why you're here. Will you tell me what happened?"

Bea turned away from Rose then spoke. "Rose, I'm not proud of killing my husband."

With a look of surprise on her face, Rose asked, "for killing your husband? You mean that was true?"

"Yes, Rose. It's no secret why I'm here. But, no one knows all the details of why. If you want to know I'll tell you. Only so you'll know there is no glory in taking another's life."

Rose sat at attention, "alright Bea, tell me everything, don't leave nothing out. I'll need to know what to expect when I put M.D. out of his misery."

Bea began her story thinking to herself that maybe this was a bad idea.

"At the time I killed my husband Rose, I didn't think about how much time I would get. I was just glad he was dead. Boy was I wrong."

"Wrong, why were you wrong Bea if he deserved it?"

"Rose, just the thought of never being a free woman again makes me want to die. I have to live with the fact daily that I took someone's life, whether he deserved it or not."

Bea paced up, and down, the 8 by 9 ft cell ringing her hands. The memories of what happened between her and her husband came back vividly.

"Back then Rose, you couldn't get help from the police if you were a battered wife. I called them many times crying and screaming for help, only for them to say, that it was a domestic dispute and not a police matter."

Rose laid down and put her hands behind her head. "Go on Bea, I'm listening."

Bea looked up at the ceiling, sighed, and then went on with her story.

"I'll never forget it. It was April 1, 1980. It was a rainy night. I had taken all I was going to take. It was bad enough I was abused by my father, but to be married to an abusive man, was more than I could bear. I prayed, please God, give me the strength to kill him if he comes at me tonight."

Rose sat on the edge of her bunk. Bea continued to tell her story.

"My pastor always said, 'be careful what you pray for,' 'cause surely that night God answered my prayer. There were two things on my side. One, he was drunk as usual, and two, he couldn't shoot. I supposed he thought it was funny, shooting at my feet to see if I would jump."

"Man Bea, that's some crazy stuff to go through."

"Well, I jumped alright, right on his back, knocking him to his knees, the gun spun out of his hand, that's when I picked it up and fired. One shot was all it took, right in the head."

Rose interrupted again, "just like I said Bea, you had no choice."

Bea looked down at the floor shaking her head.

"Rose, I never saw so much blood. I didn't panic, although I wanted to, I called the police, and told them they could come and get him now. Before the officer could give me that same speech about it being a domestic problem, I told him not to bother telling me what they couldn't do because he was dead."

Bea held her head then stopped talking. Rose sat up, prompting her to continue.

"Come on Bea don't stop there. What did you do next?"

"I called my Pastor," Bea answered.

Rose fell back on her bunk, exasperated, "you called your what?"

"You heard me right Rose, I called my Pastor."

"Bea, you just killed a man, out of all the people you could have called, why would you call your Pastor?"

"Pastor Strong knew all about the private hell I was going through with that man Rose. He never told me to leave him but, he would say that we were unequally yoked. I would laugh each time he said it, and say, pray for me Pastor, I have a weakness for men who can cook."

Bea smiled as she reminisced. "Sam was an excellent cook. He learned while in the service. I could blame my being 50 pounds overweight on him. It's been 20 years and I still can't lose it. I guess it's here to stay."

"Bea, how is your mother? How does she handle your being locked up in here?"

"She's hurting like any mother would be, blaming herself because of the way she raised me. I tried telling her it wasn't her fault; she did the best she could. Her parents were killed in a car crash you know."

"No, I didn't know Bea."

"She was only 6 and her sister was 4. They were with a sitter the day it happened. With no other known relatives to speak of, they were placed in separate foster homes. People weren't lining up to adopt two little black girls into the same home. She had only one picture of them and she kept it all those years. The picture's got to be sixty years old."

Bea stopped talking for a moment then, started to speak again, "you know Rose, I haven't heard from her lately. She usually writes me several times a month."

"Yeah, yeah," said Rose, "what happened next?"

"Rose, you did ask how my mother felt."

"Yes, I did Bea but, I didn't know you were going to go back down memory lane."

"Anyhow, the trial was quick," Bea cleared her throat, "I couldn't afford a real lawyer, with no money, so I was appointed, a public defender who didn't know what he was doing. He never mentioned at the trial how I was battered by my husband and how I continually called the police for help. Sam, with his military background, was made to look like a saint by the State's Attorney. I was wishing I had him representing me and not Gomer Pyle."

"Ha!" Rose laughed out loud, "Gomer Pyle Bea, I know that was not his name?"

"No, but, that's who he reminded me of. He had some name that sounded like cold cuts, bologna, salami, or something; anyway, the State's attorney was so good, he had me believing I was crazy."

Rose laughed again. "Bea you are crazy."

Bea laughed with her and then turned serious.

"Gomer must have thought so too, he wanted me to plead temporary insanity. I might have done better if I had represented myself."

Bea stared out into space, sitting now on the edge of her bunk.

"I knew the old saying, any man representing himself, has a fool for a client. So, there I was with my life in the hands of Gomer Pyle from Mayberry. Well, needless to say, I got life in prison for murder."

"Five minutes to lock up," a voice said over the loudspeaker.

"That's my story Rose, now you know."

"Man Bea, that's deep. I hope I'll be as cool as you were when I put M.D.'s lights out."

Bea sighed, knowing nothing she said had changed Rose's mind about killing M.D. She fell back on her bunk, "Goodnight Rose."

"Goodnight Bea, thanks for the bedtime story."

Chapter 2

In a short time, Rose and Bea had become pretty close. Bea noticed they had similar likes and dislikes. Bea grew more and more concerned with Rose's talk of how she would kill M. D. when she got out. It soon became a daily event and with her having no relationship with God she knew she would have to change her mind somehow. The few minutes before lockup became their time to talk before lights out. Rose felt like talking.

"You know Bea, did I ever tell you my grandma was my best friend?"

Bea yawned. "That's nice Rose."

"No really, she was cooler than your average grandma. She ran an escort service."

"An escort service?" Bea asked, blinking her eyes trying to focus. You mean a wh—house?"

Bea stopped before she said the actual word.

Rose laughed, "you can say it, Bea, my grandma liked to call it an escort service, she thought it sounded a lot more sophisticated. M.D. knew about it too, the dog."

The laughter in Rose's voice turned into despair when she mentioned M.D.'s name. Bea cleared her throat noticing how dry it was. She got up to get a drink of water.

"Rose, you don't have to talk about this if you don't want."

"It's okay Bea. I need to talk to someone. I've never told anyone about what happened to me and my grandma that night. Besides, who would believe me anyway?"

"I'll believe you, Rose, you don't strike me to be a habitual liar."

"You're probably the only one that would believe me, Bea."

Rose started her story again, staring out into space expressionless.

"When we met M.D., we didn't know he was a lieutenant with the Boston Police. He was treated like all the other Johns. The girls were crazy about him. He was fine, tall, and Italian, I think. When grandma found out he was a cop she gave him special favors in exchange for not closing the place down."

Bea drank her water then eased back on her bunk trying not to make any noise.

"As time went on, he not only wanted favors but, money too. Grandma paid whatever price he asked."

Bea listened closely but made no verbal response. She kept thinking to herself, what a coincidence. Rose's grandmother and my mother have the same name. She didn't comment on it. Rose stopped talking when she realized Bea was daydreaming.

"Earth to Bea, come in Bea."

Bea shook her head then apologized, "Sorry Rose I just had a little something come across my mind please, go on."

"Stay with me Bea, I don't want to have to repeat this."

Rose continued with her story.

"It got so tough my grandma couldn't pay the girls. She pleaded with him to give her a break but, he only threatened her with arrest."

Bea noticed how Rose wrung her hands as she spoke about M.D.

"I knew my grandma had a bad heart. M.D. knew it too and the added stress from him made it worse. He didn't care!"

"How did your grandmother raise you in that kind of place?"

"Oh, it was cool the girls treated me like their little sister. I was never involved in the business my Grandma saw to that. They taught me a lot. I know what to do to please a man but, I've never got the chance to test any of it out."

"What do you mean test any of it out?" You shouldn't be thinking about that kind of stuff anyway."

"Oh, come on I'm nineteen years old and you'll be pleased to know I'm still a virgin. I'm probably the only virgin in this joint."

"Well, that's good to hear Rose but, all I'm saying is, a whorehouse is no place to raise a child."

"My Grandma did the best she could raising me alone and I don't appreciate you making it sound like she was irresponsible."

"I'm sorry Rose that's not what I meant. I'm sure she did the best she could. It's just that, because of that place, you're here now."

Rose spoke, now on the defense, trying not to let her tears swell in her eyes.

"She wanted me to go to college and become a doctor, you know."

"No, I didn't know," Bea said, feeling really bad for saying what she thought.

"Not just any doctor but, a cardiologist since she had a bad heart. She would say, "Rose maybe you can find a cure for heart disease. Since nobody else had, it might as well be you." We'd have a good laugh about it. Now I'll never get the chance to go to college."

Bea added, "Rose you can still go to college. It's not too late."

"You're not hearing me, Bea." Rose's voice grew angry.

"M.D. changed all that, he'd made his own plans for me. Since my Grandma couldn't pay him like he wanted her too, he wanted me instead."

"Wanted you? Wanted you for what?"

"I guess he wanted me to turn tricks for him, I don't know but, Grandma refused, and told him she would rather die than to let him have her granddaughter. She really took a chance standing up to him like that. Her victory was short though. That same night he had the place raided. I guess being a Boston Police Lieutenant made it easy for him to arrange the bust."

Rose heard her voice crack, as her tears welled up in her eyes again.

"They arrested my Grandma right along with the other girls."

"I'm so sorry Rose."

"I was asleep when the cops broke in the door to my room and grabbed me out of bed. I didn't know what was going on, so I started to fight for my life. I grabbed the bat I kept near my bed, then swung at everything that came towards me." Rose demonstrated how she swung the bat.

"I didn't realize they were cops until it was too late, I hit one of them across the back. I swung again and broke another one's arm. You would have been proud of me Bea."

"Rose they could have really hurt you."

"Well, they wouldn't have gotten me so easy if one of them hadn't kicked me and knocked me on the floor. It took three of them to put me in the paddy wagon."

"Where was M.D. while all of this was going on?"

"That dog was there," Rose said angrily. "He watched the whole thing standing by his car smoking a cigarette like it was business as usual. He made sure we saw him before he drove off."

Tears started falling down Rose's face. She wiped them off and continued telling her story.

"When they threw me in the wagon, Grandma Jessie grabbed me and held on for dear life. She kept apologizing, saying how sorry she was, how she never meant for any of this to happen to me. She wanted me to forgive her. Before I could say anything, she grabbed her chest and had a massive heart attack."

Rose held her face and cried in her hands.

"I was helpless," she continued speaking in a small aching voice. "I tried giving her CPR, but it didn't help. By the time they got her to the hospital, she was dead."

Rose wiped her eyes again. "From that day forward I promised myself, Morton Dunn would die."

Bea's heart broke after hearing everything that happened to Rose and her Grandmother. She spoke softly.

"I am so sorry Rose. It's never an easy thing to lose a loved one. I'm sure planning her funeral was not an easy thing."

"I wouldn't know about that Bea."

"What do you mean Rose?"

"What I mean is I didn't bury my grandmother."

"Oh, you mean the state buried her?"

"No Bea, it was the strangest thing. One of Grandma Jessie's client's paid for everything?"

"Really? Who would do such a thing?"

"I don't know some guy who wouldn't give his name. I couldn't do anything being locked up and all. I really didn't want the state to bury her."

"Yes, I know what you mean. That was awfully nice of him whoever he was," said Bea.

"They set up everything over the phone with the funeral home in the area where we lived. Grandma Jessie was an old friend of his, was all he told them, it was the least he could do."

Bea scratched her head, "He sure must have liked your grandmother Rose, to do all that."

"He arranged it so I could go too but, I didn't."

Rose dropped her head and wiped another tear from her eye.

"I didn't want to attend my Grandma's funeral in chains, so I said my goodbyes from behind bars. One of the girls came to see me when I was in the city jail. She told me it was a beautiful funeral. All our old friends and neighbors were there. I'll never be able to forgive myself for not going and still to this day, I don't know who to thank."

Bea stated, touching Rose on the shoulder. "God has truly been good to you Rose."

"God? After everything that's happened to me! How can you say God's been good?"

"Rose, I know you don't understand how God works now but, one day you will, and then you'll know what I meant."

"Well, the joke must be on me because, after my trial, I was sentenced to seven years in this place, for aggravated assault on a police officer. That dog M.D. watched as they took me away."

Rose stood facing the cell bars, "tell me, Bea, where was God then?"

The guard yelled. "Lights out!"

As the lights went out in each cell, Rose stared into space, not really focusing on anything. Bea stood again, then walked over to her, and gave her a hug. Rose flinched at first and then allowed her to do so.

Bea's thoughts raced while she held Rose. I understand why she hates M.D. now but, I've got to change her mind while I have the time. Seven years may sound like a long time to some but, having to erase hatred from someone's heart, it's not long enough.

Chapter 3

"Congratulations, on your promotion Mort," said one officer.

"Congratulation old timer," said another.

One by one each officer congratulated Morton Dunn on his big promotion from Lieutenant to Captain, as he came in the doors of the station.

"I guess the last bust was all you needed, hey partner," said the officer patting Morton on his back.

"I guess," said Morton without looking at him.

Morton went into his new office then closed the door. He looked around then fell in his seat. The memory of what happened the night of the bust haunted him even now.

He realized he hadn't prayed since he was a kid. He knew God, being raised in a Catholic home, but he also felt confessing to a priest could not relieve him of the pain he felt in his heart. Just then there was a knock at the door. He stood quickly.

Morton yelled to the door. "Yeah, come in!"

One of the female officers came in. "Excuse me, Captain, there's something you should see."

Morton hurried into the outer office area, where he saw several officers crowding around a desk. He walked over to see what the matter was, that was keeping them from working. When he got close enough, the officers moved away, then yelled, "SURPRISE!"

Morton jumped and then laughed. "Hey, what is this?"

There on the desk was a huge cake, decorated, in the shape of a badge.

All of the officers sang, "For He's A Jolly Good Fellow!"

The officers beckoned him to make a speech. "Speech Capt.! Speech!" Morton cleared his throat.

"Well, all I can say is, many thanks to you all, I couldn't have come this far without your help. Because of you, I am who I am today. Thanks again."

The officers clapped. Morton waved his hands for everyone to have some cake. Even during the celebration, Morton's thoughts were filled with guilt. If they only knew what I did, he thought. They wouldn't have anything to do with me. Jessie was my friend. I loved her. How could it have gone so wrong?

"Hey Capt., aren't you going to have some of your own cake?" said Officer Jones.

Morton snapped out of his daydream. "Oh, sure Jones, I saw the piece you had, you sure don't need anymore."

Morton grabbed onto the officer's belt.

"Isn't that gut of yours begging to be set free?"

Everyone laughed.

"Hey! I've only had one piece," said Officer Jones.

"Yeah, but your one piece equals three of someone else's," said Morton while stuffing a piece of cake in his mouth.

Officer Jones tugged on his belt pulling up his pants. "I'll have you know, I've lost ten pounds on weight watchers," he said proudly.

Morton put his arm around Officer Jones's shoulder then added, "Jones the only way you've lost ten pounds is when you took off your gun and your shoes."

Everyone laughed again, even Officer Jones.

"Good one Capt.," said one of the other officers.

Morton patted Officer Jones on his back, "no offense Jones."

"None taken," replied Jones, eating his last bite of cake.

"Hey Mort, what's your first order as Captain!" yelled one of the officers.

Morton stood in the center of the room and then placed his hands on his hips.

"Alright!" He yelled. "There's a new sheriff in town! Let's get back to work, crime is not on vacation!"

"Yes sir, Captain!" answered Officer Jones while saluting.

"Get to work Jones your desk looks like a war zone," said Morton.

Morton returned to his office and closed the door.

With his head lowered, and his hands clasped together he went to his knees again and began to pray.

"Please God, forgive me for what I did to Jessie and Rose."

Tears welled in his eyes, he closed them shut.

"If you can hear me, Jessie, I'm sorry for what I did to you. I didn't mean for things to go the way they did. I know just paying for your funeral won't bring you back, or get Rose out of prison but, I promise never to use my badge for personal gain again."

He asked again, "please God forgive me."

For the first time since Jessie's death, Morton felt the heaviness of his heart grow lighter. He wiped his eyes then stood up. "Never again," he said to himself.

Chapter 4

It was approaching lockup time again. Rose and I made that our time to chat about whatever. Rose was always the first to start the conversation.

"Bea, how are you able to keep your sanity in this place after so many years?" Bea looked at Rose and asked, "my sanity?"

"Really Bea, I see how cool you are around here."

"There's no ancient Chinese secret Rose, it's because of God."

"God?" Rose rolled her eyes, "Oh, here we go again."

"Yes Rose, I know you were expecting some other answer but, without having God in my life, I would have lost my mind a long time ago from the guilt of killing my husband."

"Guilt, what guilt?"

Rose spoke with frustration in her voice. You had to kill him, Bea, to save your own life."

"I know that Rose and now you do too but, the mind plays funny tricks on you. I couldn't stop thinking that maybe I could have done something different other than killing him. With Sis. Mona's help, I was able to ask God's forgiveness."

"Forgiveness, for defending yourself?" asked Rose.

"Yes Rose, I asked God's forgiveness for taking another's man life, and He forgave me."

Rose asked, with a bit of sarcasm in her voice, "How do you know he forgave you?"

Bea noticed her sarcasm, but she didn't want to complicate things by talking too much about God so, she kept her answer simple.

"His word said so, Rose."

"His word, what word?"

"The Bible, Rose, is God's words, God's promises, everything you want to know about God is in the bible. God forgives you but, it doesn't take away the consequences of your sin.

Rose, agitated from the whole conversation asked, "consequences of your sin, now what does that mean?"

Bea explained, "for example Rose, if you slept with several men and contracted AIDS from one of them. Okay, now let's say, you accepted Christ in your life and stopped doing what you use to do, you'd still have AIDS and you'd have to deal with the consequences of having it."

Rose looked at Bea with a confused look on her face, then shrugged her shoulders. "This stuff sounds too complicated for me Bea."

Bea continued. "Many people won't turn their lives over to Christ because they don't believe they can be forgiven. I was one of them until I met Sister Mona."

"Look, Bea," said Rose, "I know I owe you a lot for helping me in here but, I don't need to be preached to."

Rose stood in front of Bea as if she was pleading her case to a jury.

"My grandma talked about God but, she never went to church, and she never made me. So, why should I bother now."

Bea listened to Rose as she continued to talk with her hands on each hip.

"I'll be out of here soon enough, and when I do, Morton Dunn will die.

"Rose I was only saying maybe Sister Mona could help you as she helped me."

"I don't need any help, Bea. You don't understand. I see why you meet with them people every week. You got nothing better to do with your time in this place. Me, I use my time thinking of different ways to kill M.D."

Bea turned away from Rose trying not to show her hurt feelings.

"You're right Rose, at first boredom was the reason why I went to church but, I know things differently now, and I would like it very much if you would go to church with me."

Rose continued to talk, now to herself as if Bea wasn't there.

She kept mumbling, "shoot him, or maybe stab him, no poison him, or maybe I'll blow up his car, kill his dog, or kill his cat, hell, I'll kill his dog and his cat. Ha! Ha! Ha! whew, I crack myself up."

Rose walked away still mumbling to herself. Bea became quite disturbed by her display. She was convinced she needed Sis. Mona's help to get Rose to turn her life over to Christ.

Chapter 5

Bea sat on her bunk feeling disgusted. She recalled the conversation she had with Sis. Mona. How could I have been so insensitive?"

"Mona?" Bea called her when no one else was around. "I've never been good at beating around the bush but, does having that hump on your back bother you? I know if I had a hump on my back, I wouldn't want to be seen."

"No Bea, it's a part of me, and it's been a part of me for a long time."

Sis. Mona joked. "God knew not to make me too fine or no one would be able to stand me." They both laughed.

"Besides Bea, I'm married to a man who loves me unconditionally. I don't have to cook or do the dishes."

"Mona, to hear you talk about the Lord, puts any natural man to shame. Well, I guess if you think about it, how can the creation be better than the creator?"

"Amen to that Sis. Bea." They both laughed.

Good thing Sis. Mona has a good sense of humor, Bea thought. I was no better than Rose asking her such a dumb question. Bea rushed to Bible class to speak to Sis. Mona before anyone else arrived.

"Mona, what am I going to do? Rose doesn't want anything to do with Bible study or church."

Sis. Mona calmly spoke, "be patient with her Bea. Remember what made you decide to start coming to Bible class?"

"Well, boredom was one reason, like I told Rose but, I always went to church when I was on the outside."

"Bea, you can't expect Rose to be filled with excitement about coming to something she's never been a part of."

"I guess," said Bea sadly. "Well, I'm not taking no for an answer. She needs God in her life and I'm going to keep at her until she says she'll come, at least once."

Sis. Mona shook her head, "alright Bea but, don't be too pushy."

Bea walked slowly back to her cell saying to herself, "don't be too pushy, don't be too pushy."

When she arrived, Rose was busily twisting her hair as she did each moment she got. Bea blurted out her question.

"So Rose, have you thought about going to bible study Wednesday?"

Rose never looked up to acknowledge she heard Bea's question.

She asked again, "Rose will you be my guest at bible study Wednesday night?"

This time Rose answered nonchalantly. "No, I don't think so, Bea."

Bea stood quietly, you're not dismissing me that easy young lady, was her thought.

On Monday and Tuesday, Bea tried to convince Rose to go with her to no avail. Each time she would say no. Bea began to become discouraged until one afternoon Rose finally reconsidered.

"God Bea, I'll go already, I'm tired of you bugging me about it."

"Very good Rose, I can't wait."

Bea didn't care how her small victory came about she was just glad it did.

She went through half the day smiling and humming. Rose found the way she was acting pretty weird.

"I'm really excited about you coming tonight Rose," said Bea.

"Bea, what's the big deal? I'm sure I'll be bored out of my mind."

Bea frowned at Rose's comment but didn't say anything.

Chapter 6

At six, Rose and Bea went to the meeting room. Everyone sat in their usual places. Rose sat in Big Bertha's chair. Before Bea could tell Rose to take another seat, in walked Big Bertha.

"OH, HELL NO!!! why is this girl in my seat?"

Big Bertha stood 6'4 an easy 300 lbs. She too was in for murdering her husband.

Big Bertha asked it again, "why is this girl in my chair!"

Rose looked up at Big Bertha real slow as if she was a tree. She put her hand up to her eyes like she was blocking the sun.

Without blinking, Rose yelled, "will somebody tell Sasquatch to get out of my face!"

Everyone knew Big Bertha could break Rose in half, but Bertha just stood there, then bent down eye level with Rose. Bertha lifted Rose up by her collar out of the chair then, she busted out with a loud laugh.

"Ha!" exclaimed Bertha, "this lil' girl got a lot of spunk! She reminds me of my lil' sister!"

She gave Rose a bear hug.

Then she told her, "you alright with me girl. You got balls! Hey everybody, meet my cousin! What's your name girl?"

Rose fell back in the chair trying to catch her breath. Breathing hard she answered, "my name is Rose."

A sigh of relief filled the room. Big Bertha sat in the seat next to Rose and gave her a big smile showing her one gold tooth with a diamond stud embedded in it. Rose looked at Bea in disbelief and shook her head.

Sis. Mona came in singing.

"Oh, how I love Je–sus," they all joined in.

Rose looked around the room. Big Bertha sang the loudest. She had a booming voice that could break the sound barrier. Sis. Mona smiled and kept on singing. Rose noticed the hump on Sis. Mona's back and couldn't stop looking at her.

Rose whispered back to Bea then giggled. "You didn't tell me Egor was teaching the class."

Bea looked at her, then frowned, "that's not funny, Rose."

Rose turned to the front, "I was just joking, Bea, lighten up."

Sis. Mona began speaking. "Thank you, ladies for lending your voices and taking time out of your busy schedules to be here tonight."

Everyone laughed, except Rose.

Rose whispered to Bea again, "what's so funny? We don't have a busy schedule in the joint."

"That's what made it funny Rose, now you lighten up," said Bea, with a grin.

"Everybody wants to be a comedian," commented Rose.

Bea laughed again at Rose's seriousness. Sis. Mona noticed them talking.

"Welcome Rose! Tell us something about yourself."

Rose looked around the room as if she wasn't talking to her, then Big Bertha spoke, "she's talking to you cuz."

Sis. Mona repeated herself, "come now Rose, stand and tell us a little about yourself."

Rose spoke abruptly. "Look, I didn't come here to give you people something to look at," she said. "I'm only here because Bea begged me to come."

Sis. Mona smiled then said, "It's alright Rose if you don't want to say anything. We're not here to make fun of anyone, or make you feel ashamed of yourself."

Rose exploded. "Ashamed! Ashamed! Why should I be ashamed? I'm in this place because a lousy cop decided to destroy me and my Grandmother's life and as soon as I get out of here, he is going to pay!"

Big Bertha yelled out, "you say it girl! Take that dog out!"

The other ladies chimed in, in agreement.

Bea hopped up. "Stop it!" she screamed, "there is still hope for Rose!" Her life is not over yet! She's only here for a short time! I can't believe the way you're urging her on like that! Talk like that is not going to get her nowhere, but back in here once she gets out!"

Rose shouted. "Be quiet Bea! Nothing you say will stop me from making M.D. pay for what he did! Besides, you're not my mother, and my grandmother is dead! So why don't you mind your own business!"

Sis. Mona slammed her Bible down on the table.

"Enough! I have stood here listening to this noise long enough! Did all of you forget why we are here?"

The guards rushed in, with their weapons drawn.

"Everything's okay officers, Sis. Mona said quickly, the ladies got a little excited. You can leave now."

Everyone stood quiet, then one by one apologized. Rose, wanted to leave too, but couldn't since the class wasn't over yet.

She mumbled to herself, "this sucks."

Chapter 7

Bea and Rose had not spoken to each other for several days. Bea finally broke their silence. "Rose, I want to show you something."

Bea lifted up her mattress, pulled out some old photos and showed them to Rose. Rose was puzzled at first, she couldn't figure out what she was looking at.

"Bea where did you get pictures of me and my Grandmother? All of these are pictures of me and my Grandma. Where did you get these?"

Rose looked at Bea waiting for an answer.

"What's going on, Bea?"

"There's something I need to tell you, Rose, please have a seat."

"I don't need to sit, Bea, what is it?"

"Then I'll sit because I don't know how to tell you this without falling down."

Bea began speaking, trying very hard to choose her words carefully.

"Rose there was something I left out of my story when I told you how I got here. It didn't seem important to tell you at the time."

"You're confusing me, Bea, what does that have to do with these pictures?"

"What I didn't tell you was, I was three weeks pregnant when they locked me up."

"Like I said, what does that have to do with me and my grandma?" Rose stated again.

Bea stared at her, then showed her letters that her Grandmother had written to her. Rose still not understanding read each letter. She sat down slowly on her bunk.

"What does this mean? This can't be," Rose said, shaking her head no.

Bea spoke quickly, "Rose your Grandmother Jessie was my mother."

Rose stopped shaking her head then stared at Bea without blinking.

"I realized after I heard your story, that your grandmother and my mother were the same person. I didn't want to believe it. I didn't want her to be dead. I felt in my heart something was wrong when I didn't get any more of her letters. I didn't know how to tell you what I thought. I knew only death would stop her from writing to me. You and she were all I had."

Bea walked over to Rose then, started to rub her hair. "Look at you. You've changed so much. I didn't even recognize my own daughter."

Rose still staring at Bea dropped the pictures on the floor.

"Daughter! Rose began to yell. "You can't be my mother! I have no mother! My mother is dead!"

Rose began to cry. Bea grabbed her, holding her, trying her best not to cry herself.

"Why didn't my Grandma tell me about you? Why did you let me grow up believing I had no mother? Why didn't you write me?"

Bea lifted Rose's head. "Rose, I'm so sorry. I asked Jessie not to tell you. I didn't even choose your name. After you were born, they took you away. It was Jessie's idea to send me pictures. Please understand why I did it this way. I'm in here for life. I will never get out unless a miracle happens."

Rose kept staring at the pictures on the floor.

Bea continued talking, "I thought it would be better if you thought I was dead, than to know your mother is a murderer, never to hold you, or be there for you when you needed me."

Rose spoke calmer now, "you could have told me anyway."

"Why Rose?" Bea asked angrily. "So, you could grow up with the embarrassment of having a mother in prison for life! And not only that, in prison for killing your father."

Rose laid in a fetal position and covered her head with her pillow. She didn't want to hear anymore. She thought to herself, this is not happening. My mother is alive. Not only is she alive but, she's in prison for life, for killing my father. After that evening Rose asked to meet with the Warden to plead with him to change her cell. Warden Powell heard what happened through prison gossip. He met with Rose upon her request.

"I won't do it, Rose, for years I've known of Bea's letters from her mother. I arranged from the beginning that you share the same cell and get to know who Bea was."

Rose said, not believing her ears. "You mean, all of you have been keeping this secret from me this whole time? Why would you do that?"

"No one else knew the two of you were related, not even Bea at first, Rose.

I felt it was best for both of you to learn who each other were, in your own time."

Rose left the Warden's office with a feeling of betrayal. Bea sat in silence looking through the pictures again thinking to herself Jessie is really dead. My mother is gone. She looked up towards the ceiling.

"Mama, thank you for taking care of Rose all these years. She's with me now. I'll do my best to take care of her while she's here."

She lowered her head, "God forgive me for not being there for her. Why did this have to happen this way?"

Bea noticed a tear fall from her eyes. She wiped it away.

"This is a real mess," she said to herself as she looked through the pictures again.

"How could I not recognize my own daughter? She's changed so much since grade school and having those locks in her hair didn't help a bit. Even her eyes are a much lighter brown than her pictures portrayed. Those old Polaroid cameras sure didn't do her any justice. She sure has come a long way from pigtails and braces."

Bea dusted the pictures off and placed them back under her mattress.

She spoke to herself again, "She may not be happy right now about this, but I'm glad to have her as my daughter. Sis. Mona will have to tell me what to do about gaining her trust again."

Bea hurriedly went to talk with Sis. Mona concerning what happened. Sis Mona had an open-door policy. She especially enjoyed Bea's company. Bea raced right in.

"Come on in Bea, I've been expecting you," said Sis. Mona dusting.

"Mona, I didn't know you were psychic too?"

"I'm not Bea, but the prison's gossip line is up and running, day and night. You know how it works."

"Well, if you know about what happened between me and Rose, then what am I going to do?"

"Give it some time Bea, she'll come around, you know that old saying, time heals all wounds."

"I pray you're right Mona, I've tried to apologize to her several times, but she won't talk to me. One thing for sure she is as stubborn as her father."

"Sis Mona stated, trying to be reassuring, "believe me when I tell you, Bea, this too shall pass, and everything will be just fine, you'll see."

Chapter 8

Morton sat at his desk quietly going through some old files that were left by the previous Captain. He decided to file them away when he ran across Rose Hill's case file. He opened it briefly, then shut it. His heart couldn't handle the guilt he felt. He thought his feelings for her had left, but he was wrong. He jumped up, went over to the file cabinet.

He mumbled to himself. "Why weren't these put away? That old coot never was very organized."

He opened the file again. The memories started coming back. He slammed the cabinet drawer closed, and sat holding his head.

"No!" he said out loud hitting his fist on the cabinet. "I said I was sorry looking up at the ceiling. "Why are you persecuting me with these memories?"

The memory of Rose and Jessie's arrest came back clearly. He made the call to have them raided. He caused Jessie's heart attack. There was no escaping that.

He talked to himself. "Why couldn't I have helped her in some other way. I could have helped her find some other line of work that was legit. I could have done something that wouldn't have caused her to die. I offered to take Rose. She misunderstood me. I loved them both. Rose was like a daughter to me. I wouldn't have harmed her. I was going to put her in medical school like she wanted. Why wouldn't she listen to me?"

Morton walked over to the window. He looked out. I can end this torture right now, he thought. He looked down. "Who am I kidding, no man dies by jumping out of a two-story window unless he falls right on his head. It'll be just my luck I'll end up crippled."

A knock came to the door. "Captain Dunn?" one of the female officers came in. Morton quickly moved over to the file cabinets and once again pulled them open.

"Mr. Culpepper gave them the slip again," said the officer.

"Who?" Morton asked trying to regroup.

The officer held up a fax from the Topeka, Kansas Police Department. "Mr. Culpepper, the embezzler, it seems he had a friend at the station when they arrested him. Somehow, he got his hands on a police uniform and, just walked out."

"What! How did they let that happen?" yelled Morton. "Idiots!" Angrily, he hit the cabinet again.

"One other thing Capt."

"What else?" Morton asked, a little calmer now.

"They think he's headed this way."

Morton rubbed his head in disgust. "Of course, he is! Put an all-points bulletin out for the guy, and make sure they have his mug shot!"

"Yes sir," said the officer as she closed the door.

Morton felt his blood pressure rise. He pulled open a lower drawer on his desk, pulled out a flask of whiskey, then took a sip. He swallowed hard smacked his lips, then put the flask away. "Well, I guess I'll have to kill myself later, much later."

Morton stood up, went back to the file cabinet. He pulled it open again. He searched through the files to find out the name of the penitentiary Rose was sentenced to. He read the name to himself, Boston Correctional Center for Women. I can't help her now, but I can keep in touch with her progress.

Chapter 9

Three years had come and gone since Rose and Bea found out they were mother and daughter. Rose's attitude had completely changed towards Bea. Bea thanked God for answered prayers. Rose hadn't talked about killing M.D. anymore once she was released from prison. Bea didn't know what to think about that. She knew she should be happy about it, but she also knew she hadn't forgotten about him.

Rose started reading and studying whatever medical books she could find concerning the heart and cardiovascular system in the prison library.

"Bea, you know, there is so much to learn about the heart, and the prison library doesn't have much on the subject. Now on the other hand, if I wanted to become a lawyer, they have everything you need to know about the law."

"Rose, I know you can do whatever you put your mind to. If you want this bad enough, you can become a doctor."

"I have to Bea, I never wanted anything so badly in my life. I made a promise to Grandma Jessie. I know I have a long way to go. One thing for sure Bea, putting me in prison has helped me get my head on straight, and that's the only thing I can thank M.D. for."

Bea seemed a bit surprised to hear Rose mention M.D.'s name. She braced herself for the other bomb to drop yet Rose had nothing else to say about him.

"Thank You, God," Bea said quietly to herself.

It wasn't long before Warden Powell noticed Rose's change himself. He walked down the corridors, heading towards their cell.

Over the years Warden Powell gained a great deal of respect from the ladies.

He nodded and spoke to each one as he passed their cell.

"Bea, I take it everything is well between you and Rose?"

Bea became startled a bit when she heard the Warden's voice.

"Warden Powell, I see they let you come out to play?" Bea said jokingly.

"I just stopped by to see my two favorite inmates."

Rose stopped reading one of the medical books she got out of the prison library long enough to say hello, then started back reading again.

Warden Powell noticed the dryness in her voice. "What are you reading, Rose?"

Rose answered quickly, "nothing."

"I see that nothing has your attention a great deal," said Warden Powell.

Bea stared at the Warden. She noticed how his hair had thinned slightly on top and she smiled. He's not such a bad man, she thought to herself. He doesn't seem to fit the role of Prison Warden though. Maybe politics would suit him better. I wish I knew his secret on how to stay in shape. He's been here as long as I have and he still looks just as good as he did when I first met him. Bea stopped daydreaming long enough to answer his first question to her. "Oh yes, Rose and I are fine, Warden."

"Very Good Bea, glad to hear."

Bea wondered the real reason why the warden was there.

"Bea our Rose has blossomed into the perfect inmate."

Rose looked up from her book to hear what else the Warden had to say.

"This is one time the prison's rehabilitation system worked."

Bea and Rose both looked at each other. Still not sure what he wanted.

"Keep up the good work Rose. I'll talk to you later Bea."

"Goodbye Warden," said Rose and Bea in unison.

Chapter 10

Shortly after lunch one of the guards came to Bea and Rose's cell.

"Rose the Warden would like to see you in his office."

Bea had a look of concern on her face then asked, "Rose did you do anything wrong?"

"No Bea, I haven't done anything wrong. Remember, the Warden said I'm a perfect inmate. Don't worry I'll be fine."

As soon as Rose left Bea fell to her knees, with her hands cupped together, "please God, don't let her be in trouble, she's been doing so good."

Rose walked into the Warden's office all smiles, looking around as if she had never been there before. She remembered the old army memorabilia all around his office. It gave the place a patriotic look, she thought. He didn't remind her of an ex-serviceman.

She said to herself, "I bet old Warden Powell got some interesting stories to tell about his past."

"Hello Rose, have a seat."

Rose thought to herself, the last time Bea asked me to have a seat and I chose to stand, she told me she was my mother.

Rose quickly took a seat and crossed her hands in her lap as if in church.

"What can I do for you, Warden?"

Warden Powell smiled, then started his speech.

"You know Rose, I've watched you closely over the years, and I must say your progress here at Boston Correctional Center for Women has been commendable. I've never seen an inmate's rehabilitation happen so quickly. You've become a model prisoner."

Rose just sat and listened. She thought it best not to say anything since she couldn't figure out where this was going.

Mr. Powell continued, "well, I want you to know that because of your good behavior the State of Massachusetts has granted you an early release from prison. Now you'll be on probation but, you'll be free."

Rose looked at him squinting. She asked slowly, "uh, Warden, did I hear you correctly?"

"You heard me, right inmate, you're going home. Here are your release papers."

Rose took the papers then read them. "My God, I never would have expected this in a million years. Thank You, Mr. Powell."

"It's my pleasure, Rose. I'm very proud of you. You'll be leaving here in one week, as soon as we clear the place you'll be staying. It's a woman's shelter run by a fine woman by the name of Ms. Weatherby. I'm sure you'll like it there. Congratulations young lady, you may go."

The guard winked at Rose then smiled and escorted her back to her cell, where Bea waited nervously.

Bea could barely contain herself, started questioning her right away. "Rose what happened? Are you in trouble?"

Rose, still in shock yelled, "I'M FREE!! Bea! I'M FREE!! I'M GOING HOME!"

Bea grabbed Rose then sat her down on her bunk, then asked slowly, "what did you say, Rose, they're letting you out?"

Rose answered in a softer voice this time, "Mom, I'm going home."

Bea looked at her with tears in her eyes then asked, "what did you call me?"

"I called you Mom, that's who you are; my mother?"

Bea grabbed Rose again this time to give her a big hug. She started to cry.

"How did this happen? You're leaving me, God Almighty. I finally have you near me and now you're leaving."

Rose looked around the cell to give Bea something to dry her eyes.

"I'm getting out on good behavior. Can you believe that Bea, on good behavior?" All I was doing was serving my time so, I could leave this place and look at what happened. God has truly smiled on me, Bea."

"That's for sure Rose," Bea said solemnly.

"Bea, I thought you would be happy for me?"

"I am happy for you Rose but, I'm going to miss you. Where will you go, now that Jessie's dead? Who will take care of you? What will you do?" Rose laughed. "Listen to you acting like a mother hen. The Warden has it all worked out. When I'm released, I'll go to a women's home and they'll find me work. Don't worry about me Ma, I'll do just fine."

It was then Rose realized herself, she wouldn't see Bea every day anymore. She hugged her again.

"I love you, Bea, thanks for not leaving me alone. I'll write every chance I get. I'm not going to lose you a second time, you're all the family I have." This time they both started to cry. At that very moment in walks Big Bertha carrying three tin cups concealed in her busts.

"What's all the boohooing about? I thought this was a celebration?"

She pulled out the cups along with a bottle of wine.

Bea asked, wiping her eyes so she could see better, "Bertha, where did you get that?"

Big Bertha replied, "let's just say, Sis. Mona's gonna have to order some more communion wine."

Bea grabbed the wine bottle, "Oh my God, you didn't?"

Big Bertha held the cups while Bea poured.

Rose added, "forgive us Lord but this sure is good." They all laughed.

Bea asked, "Bertha how did you get into that room when they keep that door locked?"

Bertha answered, "That's what's wrong with you Bea, you always gotta know what's going on. I got a hook up okay. The guard's daughter is married to my cousin's boy. Now don't say nothing 'cause I don't want you blabbering about it?"

Bea said, "Bertha you know me better than that? I didn't tell Lee Anne Brooks that it was you mooing in the shower when she was in there that day. Poor girl thinks the place is haunted by cows."

Big Bertha added, "poor girl is right, whoever heard of a prison being haunted by cows? She still won't go in the shower alone. I told you, Bea that girls got a screw loose."

Rose asked, "how did Lee Anne end up in here when she looks like she wouldn't hurt a flea."

Bea said, "it's a case of being in the wrong place at the wrong time."

Big Bertha agreed, "yeah that's what happened to me."

Bea said, "come on now Bertha you killed your husband in cold blood for sleeping with another woman."

Bertha said, "that's what I said, I was in the wrong place at the wrong time when the police caught me."

"You'd better get back to your cell before they catch you again with this wine," said Bea shooing her out.

Rose couldn't help but laugh. "Thanks, Bertha, for the wine.

Rose then gave Big Bertha a hug.

"I won't forget you cuz!" yelled Bertha, looking as if she would cry. "Give 'em hell when you get out."

"Bertha don't' tell her that," exclaimed Bea.

"Come on Bea, I meant that in a Christianly way."

Bertha turned and winked at Rose before leaving. Rose laughed.

Bea shook her head with disapproval, "Rose, that woman need lots of prayers."

Chapter 11

Bea watched as Rose packed up what little belongings she had before leaving. She felt happy and sad at the same time. Rose tried not to notice her holding back her tears. She kept the conversation as light as possible.

"Now when I'm gone, all of this will be yours," said Rose.

Bea smiled.

"Come on now Ma, you promised no more tears."

Bea spoke slowly, "you know, Rose I believe I'm the only woman who ever got a chance to be a mother to her own daughter while in prison. Talk about getting a second chance. If anyone ever tries to tell me what God can't do, they got a fight on their hands."

"Amen to that, Pastor Bea!" Rose laughed.

"I'm going to miss you so much Rose, but I'm glad you're not going to be here anymore. You too have a second chance."

"Don't worry Ma, I'll be fine."

Rose gathered her things then asked Bea not to walk out with her. She couldn't stand to see her cry again. Bea hugged her one last time.

"Goodbye Rose, don't forget me."

Rose walked down the corridor to be let out, just as proud as she did when she walked in. This time she walked proudly for different reasons. She had a mother, and she had God.

"Goodbye Rose, we'll miss you," said Lee Anne.

The other ladies said goodbye one by one as she walked by their cells. Rose waved, feeling somewhat like a celebrity.

Big Bertha stood by Lee Anne and mooed as Rose walked by.

Rose laughed, "behave yourself, Bert."

"Ain't no fun in that," snickered Big Bertha.

Lee Anne looked around frightened as ever, then ran back to her cell.

Big Bertha whispered to Rose, "I told Bea, that girl wasn't all there?"

Rose laughed again. "Goodbye Bertha, take care of my mama."

"You know it, Rosie,"

"And don't call me Rosie."

Big Bertha laughed.

Sis. Mona waited for Rose near the gate. Rose gave her a hug.

"Thank you for everything Sis. Mona, I'll never forget you."

"No matter what happens Rose, don't forget that God is always there. Just call whenever you need Him. You'll see, you're never alone."

Sis. Mona grabbed Rose by the arm. "Rose, I've been meaning to ask you. What brought about such a drastic change in you towards Bea and God when you were so angry?"

"You know, Sis. Mona, I was very angry at Bea at first for not telling me she was alive. The more I thought about it, the more I understood why she did it. I wasn't angry at God. I didn't know him but, over the years I've gotten to know him and become closer to him. Now I know he's been watching over me all this time and it was not by coincidence that I would find my mother right after my grandmother had died. That had to be divine timing."

Sis. Mona hugged Rose again. "I'm so proud of you, Rose. I'll miss you.

Rose kissed her on the cheek then started walking toward the guard.

"As soon as you get settled, find a church and join it, the fellowship will do you good!"

"I will," said Rose.

Rose collected the money she had earned while in prison and signed out. The familiar words, "Open the Gates!" rang out.

Rose started out, turned, and gave the place one last look. I'm free! she thought, Praise the Lord I'm free! She started singing to herself as she walked towards the bus, remembering one of the old Negro hymns she found in Sis. Mona's hymn book.

"I'm free, praise the Lord, I'm free

No longer bound, no more chains holding me

My soul is resting, It's such a blessing

Praise the Lord, hallelujah I'm free."

The bus ride to town was a bumpy one. Rose was amazed at how things hadn't changed much in 3 ½ years. It was as if time stood still. People still wore the same clothes, the same hairstyles. I guess 3 ½ years is not a long time Rose thought, but to lose it being locked up in prison, that's when it's too much. She felt a rumble in her stomach.

She said to herself, "I can't remember the last time I felt hunger pains. One thing they did do, in the joint was feed you even if you didn't like it. I can't wait to get to my new home. God, I wish Bea was here with me."

When the bus arrived at the depot Rose said a silent prayer. "Please God, let me make it this time. I've got to."

Chapter 12

Holding on to her bags, she stepped off the bus feeling like a tourist. Just then a young lady walked up holding a sign with Rose Hill's name written on it. She walked over to Rose and said, "excuse me, are you Rose Hill?"

Rose answered, "I am."

The young lady introduced herself. "My name is Candy. I'm here to take you to Farmington House."

"Hello Candy, Rose said as she looked around. "Where is Ms. Weathersby?"

"Ms. Weathersby sent me to meet you. She runs the place. She never comes out herself. We knew you were coming last week. I hope you had a good ride?"

Rose followed along, while Candy continued her conversation.

"I was born at Farmington House. My mother died giving birth to me there. They tell me no one knew she was pregnant. I guess you can say Ms. Weathersby's my mother, she raised me."

Rose thought to herself, how does she talk that much without taking a breath. She's like that bunny, that keeps going and going. She seems to be pretty friendly, though. I hope all the other ladies aren't chatty like her. I won't be able to stand it if they all talk that much.

"We're here Rose. What do you think?"

Rose looked up at the red brick building with green vines crawling up and down its sides. Not much to look at she thought, but it's still better than being in prison. I'll just have to make the best of it.

Ms. Weathersby came out to greet her. Rose didn't know what to expect. She marveled at how Ms. Weathersby looked like a younger version of her Grandma Jessie.

"I wonder if she could be related somehow," Rose said to herself.

I'd better get my foot in the door first before I start questioning her about her family tree. It would be nice to know, if I had more family other than Bea, Rose thought to herself.

Rose shrugged her shoulders then walked up closer to the porch.

"I can only hope; this being alone out here is not a good feeling," she mumbled to herself.

Patrice, Violet, and Stacey came out to greet her. Rose shook their hands sizing up each one in her mind. Prison had taught her how to do that.

Patrice taller and slimmer than the other two came out first. Rose thought long hair, definitely not hers. I'm sure she calls the shots with the other girls. Violet, short, stocky, not very friendly, seems to have a chip on her shoulder. Stacey, pretty girl, nice, giggles a lot though, reminds me of Lee Anne back in the joint.

She remembered the cold shoulder she gave Bea when she met her the first time. She was careful not to do the same thing here.

"Thank you all for coming out to greet me, I'm sure I'll like it here," said Rose trying not to sound phony.

Ms. Weathersby waved her hand for Patrice and the other ladies to step aside.

"Come on in Rose, I'll show you to your room. Here are some clean linen and towels, you can tend to them later. The rules of the house are simple: You dirty it, you clean it."

Rose laughed when she saw the sign hanging over the fireplace.

Ms. Weathersby continued, "it may seem juvenile to have a sign such as this one Rose, but we don't need a bunch of rules in this place. Everyone has a job to do and goals to reach. My job is helping you reach those goals, as long as they're obtainable."

Rose smiled in agreement.

"We'll talk later, right now get cleaned up for dinner. We have an excellent cook here, his name is Vincent Hamlin, and he's been with Farmington House for 15 years now.

Ms. Weathersby counted her fingers to confirm her accuracy. "Yes, it's been about 15 years. It sure doesn't seem that long."

Ms. Weathersby stopped talking and went into deep thought.

Rose noticed Ms. Weathersby's hesitation and started to giggle. She thought to herself, she goes off into la-la land just like Bea when she tells a story.

Rose's giggles broke Ms. Weathersby's trance.

"Oh, I'm sorry Rose, where was I?" asked Ms. Weathersby.

"You were talking about Vince's cooking."

"Ah yes, I remember now. Vince takes pride in his cooking. He prepares a special dinner whenever a new member joins the family. He doesn't like us to come to dinner late. He says food should be eaten while it's hot. He never liked warming food in a microwave oven. I guess he's old fashioned that way."

Rose thought to herself hot or cold, I'm sure whatever he fixes will be triple better than what they served in the joint.

When they got to the dining area, everyone was already seated.

Ms. Weathersby commented, "you see Rose, if you want a seat, you can't drag your feet."

Everyone laughed.

Candy whispered to herself, "I can't believe that line still gets a laugh."

Ms. Weathersby chuckled, "Candy pipe down and slide over so Rose can sit next to you."

Rose stared at the beautifully set table covered with so much food that she didn't know what to try first. She gazed from one end of the table to the other. Glazed ham with yams, roast duck, stuffing, giblet gravy, mashed potatoes, collard greens, corn bread, fried green tomatoes, lamb chops, homemade lemonade and for dessert, pineapple upside down cake with whipped cream.

Rose licked her lips then whispered to Candy. "He must have been up all night preparing this much food. I hope it tastes as good as it looks."

Candy whispered back, "Vince is an excellent cook. He says cooking is his way of expressing himself."

"Yoo-hoo, Rose!" yelled someone, from the far end of the table.

Rose looked down to see where the voice came from. An older woman looked to be in her late seventies waved to her.

"Hi! I'm Clara, I missed you coming in. I'm the secretary for Farmington House. I'm sure Willie was going to bring you around to meet me eventually, right, Willie?"

Rose nudged Candy, "who is Willie?"

Candy whispered, "Willie is Ms. Weathersby. Don't ever call her that, she hates it. She said her father gave her and her sister boys names, 'cause he wanted boys. That's all she would say about her family. She's always been really private about it. The only person here who can call her Willie, is Ms. Clara and that's because she's older."

Ms. Clara asked again, "I know you were going to bring her around eventually to meet me, weren't you, Willie?"

Ms. Weathersby mumbled when she said her name again. "I heard you the first time you old bat." She then answered louder. "Yes, Clara, I was going to bring her around to meet you after dinner!"

Ms. Weathersby stood up, then leaned on the table.

"Now, is there anyone else who has not met Rose?" No one said another word. Alright then let's eat. Ms. Weathersby yelled to the kitchen door, "Vince, come out and be seated!"

He yelled back, "I'll eat in the kitchen if it's alright!"

Candy nudged Rose, "wait 'till you meet Vince."

Ms. Weathersby got up from the table, sighed, and then went into the kitchen. Candy jumped up and raced to the door, putting her ear against it. Quickly she sat back in her seat.

"I couldn't hear a thing."

Ms. Weathersby returned and took her seat. "Everyone, Vince will be joining us after all."

The kitchen door opened slightly. Out came a young man in his middle twenties. Rose's mouth flew open as she checked him out from head to toe. She noticed he wore his hair in locks just like hers. His eyes were big and brown, and she noticed he needed a shave. Poor thing, he's probably been up cooking all morning she thought. Rose felt herself staring so, she tried looking away, but her eyes fell back on him. His chef's jacket fell slightly open when he sat. Rose could see part of his chest.

"Look at that chest," Rose whispered. "I thought he was an old man the way Ms. Weathersby talked about him."

Candy whispered back to Rose, "I forgot to mention that Vince, short for Vincent was fi-ine but, he's like a brother to me so, he's no big deal."

Rose whispered back to Candy, "speak for yourself, he's not just fine, he's gorgeous. What's his story?"

Candy answered, "I don't think he's into his looks. All he does is cook and work out."

"He could be a model," said Rose.

Patrice butted in, "he could model for me anytime. By the way, my name is Patrice in case you forgot."

"Yes, I know, we met on the porch," said Rose.

Candy whispered again. "Watch her Rose, she can't be trusted. She's been after Vince for a long time now. He won't give her the time of day. And don't loan her any money."

"Don't worry, I don't have any money to loan," said Rose.

"Well, when you do don't loan her any or you won't get it back."

Rose felt her stomach growl again. She volunteered to bless the food.

Ms. Weathersby said, "please do Rose, it's about time somebody else gave God some thanks around here."

Everyone bowed their heads except Vince. He watched Rose all the while she gave the blessing, smiling as if she was talking to him. No one noticed Vince watching her but, Ms. Weathersby and she was not pleased.

Chapter 13

After dinner, everyone helped with clearing the dishes. Ms. Clara fell asleep at the table.

"I'll wash the dishes, Ms. Weathersby," said Patrice while stacking the plates on the table.

Violet grabbed up the saucers, "I'll help you, Patrice."

Stacey added, "I might as well help too."

Ms. Weathersby, unimpressed by their offer, said, "that's okay ladies, Rose, Candy, and I will do the dishes tonight, you three see to the laundry."

Patrice protested, "Ms. Weathersby, why won't you ever let us wash the dishes for you?"

"Patrice, I know you mean well but, poor Vince wouldn't stand a chance against you girls in that kitchen."

Violet and Stacey laughed, then gave each other a high five, "you know it," they both said in unison.

Patrice didn't appreciate Ms. Weathersby's insight. She huffed, and turned to leave, beckoning for Violet and Stacey to come with her.

Rose grabbed the stack of dishes from the table while Candy collected the glasses and flatware. Rose went into the kitchen door just as Vince was about to come out.

CRASH!! All the plates dropped from her hands onto the dining room floor. Ms. Clara jumped, opened her eyes, then closed them again.

Rose screamed, "Oh No, Vince! I didn't see you coming out. I'm so sorry."

Ms. Weathersby remained calm about the whole incident. Right away, she started calculating out loud how much Rose owed for the broken plates and saucers.

"Let's see, eight plates, three dollars each, eight saucers, two dollars each. Well, Rose, it seems you owe Farmington House forty dollars for dishes."

Rose protested, "but Ms. Weathersby, it was an accident!"

While holding the door open for Candy to bring in the last of the dishes, Ms. Weathersby added, "I'm sorry dear, but there is one other rule I failed to mention we have in this house and that is; If you break it! You buy it!"

Vince quickly got the broom and dustpan to help Rose clean up the broken pieces. He stooped down just as she did and knocked her over. The pieces fell from her hands onto the floor once again.

Rose spoke, feeling a bit agitated, "Vince, please let me do it myself before I buy something else."

"Don't you worry about Ms. Weathersby; I'll talk to her. She's all bark and no bite," said Vince.

Vince held his hand out to Rose to help her up, and she grabbed his hand and part of his arm for balance. He pulled her up in one swoop when their eyes met.

Rose commented, "handsome, and strong."

Vince blushed, almost letting her go. He quickly apologized. "I'm sorry. I've been telling Ms. Weathersby that door needs a window. I knew someday this would happen."

Rose, noticing his accent asked, "Where are you from, Vince?"

"Why, I'm from London, London, England," said Vince.

"I've never met anyone from London before. You sure are a long way from home, aren't you?"

"Not really, this is my home," Vince said with a sigh.

Ms. Weathersby came out of the kitchen abruptly, startling Rose.

"Okay now Rose, Vince, there are still plenty of unbroken dishes left to wash. You all finish up. I'll put Ms. Clara to bed. I won't leave her to find her own room. I hate to bother her since she's sleeping so soundly."

Ms. Weathersby shook Ms. Clara to wake her, "come on Clara time to go to bed."

Before going into the kitchen, Vince grabbed Rose's arm. "Thank you for helping with the dishes."

Rose smiled, "I have to do something to earn my keep around here."

Vince asked Rose, "would you like to come up to my room and talk sometimes?"

"Sure, if you like," said Rose.

Vince whispered closer now in her ear, "I like."

Rose felt it refreshing to have a man talk to her that close, and it not be a cop or prison guard. She giggled.

Candy saw the whole thing. "Ooo," she exclaimed, "no you didn't just get here and already got the untouchable Vincent Hamlin panting after you. He's never shown any interest in the other girls here. We thought he was gay. Wait until I tell Patrice and the others."

Rose knew if Candy said anything about what she saw, there would be trouble.

She spoke up quickly, "Candy I'm sure Vince isn't interested in me, but if he is, I just got here, and I don't want any trouble. Promise me you won't say anything?"

Candy agreed under protest. "I finally get something juicy to tell, and I have to keep it to myself."

"Thanks, Candy, I owe you one."

Chapter 14

Morton showered, feeling a little better than he had. Knowing Rose was now out of prison made him feel good. He made himself some coffee and looking around his condo, he noticed how untidy everything was.

"This place is a mess," he said out loud like he was waiting on someone to respond.

He removed a slice of bread from its wrapper to find it was molded.

"I must be slipping. When did I buy this?"

He threw the bread in the wastebasket. "I guess this is what depression does to you. I've got to get myself together. I can't be of any help to Rose this way."

He sipped some coffee, turned the television to the local news. He thumbed through his mail which had piled up on the counter. After noticing the time, he hurried to his bedroom, grabbed his uniform, and quickly dressed.

"I can't tell the officers to be on time if I'm late."

He ran out the door to the elevator and pressed the down button.

"Mr. Dunn! Mr. Dunn! I'm still waiting for you to join me for dinner. You know you have an open invitation."

Morton cringed when he heard his neighbor's voice.

"Come on elevator," he mumbled while pushing the down button again.

"Mr. Dunn! I'm waiting!"

"Yes, I know Ms. Jackson, I've been pretty busy."

Morton pressed the elevator button again. Frustrated, he mumbled, "where is the elevator?"

Ms. Jackson came out into the hall wearing a silk robe with high heel slippers. She allowed her robe to fall off one shoulder, showing she had nothing on underneath. Her red hair hung long and combed over to one side. She walked quickly up to him and backed him up against the elevator door. Running her finger up and down his mouth, she spoke.

"Why Mr. Dunn, are you sure you don't want to come over for dinner tonight?"

"Sorry Ms. Jackson, maybe some other time. Right now, I have to go to work."

"Maybe, I can keep something a little hot for you until you get in."

Ms. Jackson rubbed her hand up and down her inner thigh. She reached for Morton's belt buckle, just as the elevator doors came open. Morton stopped himself from falling into the elevator. Ms. Jackson stumbled with him, dropping her robe to the floor. Morton grabbed her robe and handed it to her.

"For Pete's sake! Ms. Jackson put your robe back on! I'm late for work!"

Morton stepped in the elevator and pressed the button for the door to close. Ms. Jackson stood in the hall and stared as the doors closed in disbelief. "Your loss," she huffed and then walked back to her condo.

Chapter 15

The next morning, Ms. Weathersby met with Rose to discuss her plans at Farmington House. She was quite impressed to hear Rose wanted to go to Medical School.

"Now don't misunderstand me, Rose, at Farmington House, we want all of you ladies to reach your highest goals possible but, to become a doctor? I don't know."

Ms. Weathersby walked over to an old bureau and straightened a picture frame.

"We don't have that kind of money to send you to Medical school, and for who knows how many years?"

Rose began pleading her case, "I know it won't be easy, Ms. Weathersby and I'm not looking for a free ride but, I have to try. I'll do whatever it takes. I can work during the day and, go to school at night. It'll probably take a long time, but it's what my grandmother wanted.

"With your determination and lots of self-discipline, I believe you can do it, Rose. Oh, and by the way, we found you some work," Ms. Weathersby smiled.

"Already!" I just got out. How did you do that?"

"It wasn't hard, the Mid-town Nursing Home is always hiring. They're not paying much but, it's a start. The director has a good heart. Her name is Mrs. Patty Wilson. She has hired ladies from Farmington House before, and I must say it's been quite successful for many of them. Patrice also works there. Mrs. Wilson is expecting you today."

"This is great, Ms. Weathersby! I didn't expect to find work this fast."

Rose memorized the address then put the paper in her pocket.

"Once you get there you can work out your hours with her. Now don't let me down."

"Thank you, Ms. Weathersby, I won't let you down and "thank you, God," she said silently.

Rose thought of Ms. Weathersby and Grandma Jessie resembling each other once again. Rose walked toward the door. She noticed the yellow pages on the table next to the phone. She picked it up, turned to the churches.

"There are so many," she said, shuffling through the pages. "Which one do I choose?" Disgusted Rose slammed the book shut.

Her mind began to wander. God, how I miss Bea and even Big Bertha. I promised Sis. Mona, I would find a church home. I have no idea where to look. I've never been to a church outside of prison.

She put the book back on the table. Vince peeked his head out of the kitchen door.

"Psst! Rose," Vince beckoned for her to come over.

Rose walked over with a look of surprise on her face. "Good morning Vince, I'm sort of in a hurry and why are you whispering?"

She thought to herself how handsome he was, and how the ladies that worked for her grandma would have eaten him up. She rubbed her stomach. Why does my stomach feel funny when I see him? I'm not used to this. Rose remembered what Sis. Mona taught her; pray about everything. She wanted to do so right then but felt a bit embarrassed with him standing there. She shut her eyes instead and prayed a silent prayer.

Vince stepped out of the kitchen door and stood in her face, "did you include me in your prayer?"

Rose jumped back. "What are you doing?"

"I just wanted to say good luck on your first day of work."

Rose quickly regained her composure. "Why Mr. Hamlin have you been eavesdropping? How did you know where I was going?"

"I know where everyone goes in this place," he said.

Oh, you're Farmington House security, huh?" Rose laughed.

"Very funny Rose, but it's kind of hard to keep secrets here."

Rose turned to leave. "Thank you for your well wishes, but I've got to go, or I'll be late for my first day."

Rose walked at a fast pace down the hall towards the door, thinking of Vince. She was not really sure what to make of him but, she did want to get closer. Out of nowhere appears Candy with a big smirk on her face.

Rose asked, "Candy, how long have you been standing there?"

"Oh, just long enough to see you two are up to something," answered Candy with a giggle.

This time Rose felt a little exasperated with the whole thing.

"We're not up to anything Candy, shouldn't you be in school?"

Candy chuckled, "don't mean to burst your bubble but, I'm out of school for the summer. You don't have to worry about me Rose, it's none of my business what you and Vince do. I know one thing Patrice, and the others are not going to like it."

Feeling the need to defend herself, Rose stated, "Candy, Vince and I have done nothing wrong. As far as Patrice and the others not liking something; I'm happy to say they have neither a heaven nor a hell to put me in." Rose went out the door and slammed it behind her. Candy stood, staring at the closed door. "Well, excuse me for breathing," she said, before going upstairs.

Chapter 16

Rose walked briskly to the Nursing Home just three blocks away, trying not to be late. She thought to herself, Mid-town Nursing Home what an unoriginal name, even though it is in the middle of town. When she got to the building, she stopped to look over its architecture.

"What a dump," she said. "This old place should be torn down. How can they have people living here?"

Rose noticed the cars parked around the side and the back of the building.

"There sure are a lot of cars parked around here. I wouldn't leave my car around this dump."

She looked around more. "I'd better stop talking to myself before someone thinks I'm a resident."

When she walked inside the place, Rose frowned on the horrid conditions the home was in. The paint was peeling everywhere, the woodwork coming away from the walls, light bulbs out in some of the hall corridors. Rose approached the Nurse's station, "excuse me, where is Mrs. Wilson's office?"

The Nurse didn't bother to look up, she just pointed toward a door down the hall.

"Thank you, Ms. Personality," Rose muttered.

She then walked toward the door. Once there, she read the sign Patty Wilson Director, on the door.

She knocked, then a voice on the other side of the door said, "come in."

Rose walked in, trying not to notice how dim the lights were.

Mrs. Wilson turned around in her chair to face Rose, who's there?" she asked.

Rose didn't know Mrs. Wilson was blind. "Hi, I'm Rose Hill. Ms. Weathersby told me to come over for a job."

Mrs. Wilson held her hand out for Rose to shake. "Hello Rose, that's a nice name. Have a seat.

Rose said, "I'm sorry I didn't know you were blind. She mumbled under her breath. "Ms. Weathersby should have mentioned that."

Mrs. Wilson said, "don't apologize, Rose, I've been blind since birth. I've never known what light looks like. I can only imagine. Now enough about me, what about you. Ms. Weathersby told me you were coming and that you were eager to work. Now, I'm not a hard person to get along with. Whatever hours you're able to work, I'm sure we can work something out."

Rose notice a picture of both Mrs. Wilson and a distinguished looking man behind her desk.

"Is that your husband?" Rose asked.

Mrs. Wilson stopped talking, then stood up and touched the picture.

"Ah Yes, that was my husband Bill, God rest his soul. He truly believed in Farmington House, and so do I. They'll always have my support."

Mrs. Wilson turned then sat down again.

"When he died, I took over the place. The state doesn't contribute much funding to this place. The majority of our funding comes from the residents who live here, most of them don't have families, and those who have families never visit. This place was so full of life when my husband was alive."

Rose heard the despair in Mrs. Wilson voice. "Mrs. Wilson, I will help in any way I can. Am I hired?"

"Of course, you're hired, Rose. We'll start you on the early shift next week nine 'til five."

Rose asked, "Mrs. Wilson why does the place look so run down?"

Mrs. Wilson, sat up in her chair then leaned forward, "run down? What do you mean run down?"

Rose was not sure if she should say anymore. She knew now, Mrs. Wilson did not know the condition her Nursing Home was in. Rose told her what she saw from the time she walked in the building to the walk down the corridor. Mrs. Wilson shook her head with disbelief.

"None of the other girls ever said a word. Why wouldn't they tell me?"

She looked as if she would cry. "All this time I thought everything was fine. The Board always had doubts I could run this place without Mr. Wilson, I guess they were right."

Rose stood up and gave her a hug.

"I'm so sorry, Mrs. Wilson. I didn't mean to hurt you. I don't know why the other girls didn't tell you, but I'll do everything I can to help you."

"Thank you, Rose, I'm glad you're here. I'll have one of the girls show you around. Give me a moment, and I'll call someone at the nurse's station."

"That's not necessary, Mrs. Wilson I'll give myself a tour if you don't mind."

"Okay Rose, just ask Linda at the nurse's station to give you a name tag."

Rose hesitated. "Before I leave Mrs. Wilson, can I pray with you?"

Mrs. Wilson smiled, "sure Rose,"

Rose prayed then left.

Chapter 17

After the meeting with Mrs. Wilson, Rose walked down the hall. She heard a noise coming from behind a door that read laboratory. Just as she was about to put her ear up to the door to listen. Patrice came out.

"Well, hey girl, I see you made it."

"Yes, I did. Why didn't anyone tell me Mrs. Wilson was blind?"

"Well, I don't know why Willie didn't tell you, but it sure helps," said Patrice."

"Helps," what do you mean helps? And why are you calling Ms. Weathersby, Willie?"

"Look, girl, what that old crow don't know won't hurt her," said Patrice.

Rose turned toward the lab door again. "What's going on in there?"

Patrice stepped in front of her and said, "oh girl, don't worry about that. That's just old man Henry screaming 'cause he doesn't want an enema."

Rose said, "that doesn't sound like a man screaming. I know I haven't been around much, but it sounds like a wheel turning, and a ball rolling around like in a casino."

Patrice pointed her finger in Rose's face. "Now look you! I don't know who you think you are but, don't start putting your nose somewhere it doesn't belong!"

At that very moment, a huge man came out of the door.

"Anything wrong, Patrice," he asked?

"I don't think so Bo," said Patrice. She turned to look at Rose, "is there anything wrong, Rose?" Rose looked at the 7-foot giant and remembered Big Bertha. She began to smile.

"Why hello there Bo, aren't you a big guy." Rose smiled again. Bo blushed. Rose held her hand out for Bo to shake, then introduced herself. "Hello again, I'm Rose Hill. I'm new here."

Just as they were about to shake hands, Patrice broke in.

"This girl was trying to say something is going on in here Bo." Patrice rolled her eyes and folded her arms.

Bo said, now trying to look serious, "look Rose there's nothing to see here," then stood in front of the door.

Rose smiled again, "okay, I'll just give myself a tour of the place since I'll be working here."

Rose walked down the hall with her hands behind her back, looking around. She turned to see if Patrice was watching, but they had already gone back inside the room. She quickly ran back up the corridor to the lab door then placed her ear to the door. Being very still, she listened.

"I know casino noise when I hear it," Rose whispered to herself. This explains why there are so many cars parked around here. How could they get away with this, she thought?

Rose grew angrier as she listened.

She thought; I know Patrice couldn't pull this off by herself. There's got to be a money man behind all this, I wonder who it is? That dirty cow, she would be a part of something like this and be on parole too.

Rose looked up to the ceiling. "God, why me? Why did I have to find out? Why did I have to promise Mrs. Wilson I would help her? Me and my big mouth."

Linda, the nurse, walked up to Rose and tapped her on the shoulder. Rose nearly bumped her head on the door.

"Shish, don't make a sound. Come with me," whispered Linda.

Linda then grabbed Rose by her arm and pulled her in the room across the hall.

Rose started to ask Linda did she know what was going on in the lab when Linda cut her off.

"I'm an undercover police officer. I've been undercover here as a nurse, watching the place for months. I pretend like I don't see anything, and that allows them to let their guards down all the time around me."

Rose couldn't believe her ears. She was involved with the police again.

"Patrice is only a small piece in this racket. We want the man behind it all, said Linda. "It takes a lot of money to set up something like this. And that's why we can't have you blowing things for us."

"I don't believe this I haven't been out a week and, already I'm in the middle of a police investigation. Bea would just die if she knew I was involved with the police again."

Rose shook her head as if trying to wake up from a bad dream.

"Look, Rose, we know you're not a part of this but, we will need your help."

"My help? How can I help the police?"

Linda put her hands over Rose's mouth and began whispering.

"You must play along with them, get closer, we need someone they will trust to let in their little clubhouse. I can only go so far. I can't get in the room without breaking in and blowing my cover. They keep the door locked, and Bo keeps me away when it's not."

Linda peeked out the door to see if anyone was coming.

"I've questioned them on what's going on in there but, I got the same response you did. Bo wasn't as nice to me as he was to you. That seven-foot gorilla, he'll be the first one I'm gonna bust when we finally get the evidence we need. Mrs. Wilson calls him one of her best workers. Poor thing. My guess is things went sour when the old man died. She's going to be devastated when she finds out."

Rose asked, "what will happen to Mrs. Wilson?"

"Nothing will happen to her but, they will shut this place down."

"This place is all she has left of what she and her husband built together. You just can't close it."

"Rose that's not my call I'm afraid. But her place does harbor criminal activity and look at the condition it's in? I like, Mrs. Wilson, however, she should not have to run a place like this alone."

Rose said, trying to defend Mrs. Wilson, "she wasn't alone until her husband died. I'm sure she thought she had capable help in place. Look at you, you're a cop, pretending to be a nurse. Patrice is supposed to be working here too, and she's a crook. No wonder the place is falling apart. I can only imagine what her books look like. How can they run a casino in such a small place?"

"All they need Rose is a couple of slot machines, a blackjack table, a dealer, some dice, then presto, a mini casino. Believe it, Rose, people use all kinds of places for gambling, but this is my first nursing home casino."

"How are their customers getting in and out if they're not using this entrance?"

"That's what we'll need you to find out for us Rose."

"Me? I just got out. I don't want any part in this."

Just then, the door from the lab opened. Both Linda and Rose listened carefully to hear who was coming out or going in. Linda cracked the door, only to hear a familiar voice.

"I know who that is; he sure has a lot of confidence in himself. He just knows no one is watching him."

Rose trying to peek through the crack in the door whispered, "Linda, who are you talking about?"

"Sorry Rose," said Linda now shutting the door.

"I'm talking about, Mr. Culpepper the Nursing Home's accountant. He comes in twice a week. I assumed it was to do the books. I would have never guessed. He was so quiet, barely said anything to anyone except hello. I've got to see what's in those books?"

Rose asked, "how can you do that without him catching you?"

"Oh, that'll be easy, they're so lax," said Linda. "They'll never know what hit 'em. I'll call in and get a thorough rundown on our Mr. Ernie Culpepper. It won't be long now, Rose."

Rose shook her head in disgust, "why me?"

Linda laughed, "Don't worry Rose, you'll be alright. We've already checked you out. We're only concerned about the people involved in this scheme. We know you were released from prison. We're not trying to send you back." Your parole officer will be notified about the whole situation and how we will need your help with this case."

Rose sighed, "that's a relief."

"We know about all the ladies that work here. Too bad some of them will be going back to the pen."

Linda cracked the door again to see if the coast was clear to leave out. They both hurried to the front desk.

"Okay now Rose, you go on. I'll report into headquarters and let them know what we found out when the coast is clear. Patrice will be getting off work soon. She'll be coming to sign out even though she's done no real work."

Linda made the phone call she needed before Patrice came out of the lab. She gave Mr. Culpepper's name and description to headquarters. It wasn't long before they contacted her back to confirm who Culpepper really was. The officer, on the other end of the phone, quickly spoke. "I believe we're talking about the same guy Linda. He goes by several aliases and was arrested for embezzling a few hundred thousand dollars from a couple of Financial Trust Companies in the Mid-West three years ago. He's been on the run ever since. We wondered where he'd end up."

"Thanks, Manny let the Captain know what we have found. I'll await further orders."

Linda quickly hid her cell phone in her sweater pocket. She walked by the lab door then thought to herself, have all your fun now guys, the party is almost over. All I need now is to get a peek at the nursing home financial records to see if Culpepper is skimming money to fund his casino. Linda knew that wouldn't be easy to do and she would have to get Rose to help her.

Chapter 18

Rose left the nursing home shaken a bit. This could only happen to me, she thought. When she returned back to Farmington House, she quietly went to her room. She was happy no one was around, especially Vince. She didn't bother going down for lunch. Rose wished she could talk to Bea and get some advice, but she knew she couldn't, being an ex-con.

She told herself, "I can write to Sis. Mona and she can tell Bea and the others how I'm doing. I don't see any harm in that. I surely won't mention the mess I'm in. It would only make Bea worry."

Rose sat down to gather her thoughts. "There's plenty I can write about without telling everything, she said to herself again. She wrote about her trip, the girls, Ms. Weathersby and how she resembled Grandma Jessie, and of course, she told them about Vince. She wrote until she got writer's cramp. Feeling tired, she fell asleep.

Two hours later, Candy knocked on the door. "Are you in there, Rose, it's me Candy?"

"Come in Candy," said Rose sleepily.

"Hi Rose, dinner's ready, you know you better get down there before Ms. Weathersby comes up."

"I'll be right down Candy; I'll just need to freshen up a bit."

Rose went down to dinner and sat next to Candy.

Ms. Weathersby asked, "Rose, will you say grace?"

Patrice didn't bow her head this time, she watched Rose as she prayed. Rose kept her grace short this time.

Ms. Weathersby asked, "you seem a little far off Rose how did it go at the Nursing Home?"

Patrice looked at Rose with a worried stare on her face.

Rose smiled. "Oh, it was fine. I really like Mrs. Wilson. It would have been nice if someone had told me she was blind."

"Would it have made a difference Rose if you knew ahead of time that she was blind?"

"Well no, but it would have made it a little less awkward."

"For you, or for her," chuckled Clara.

"That's enough Clara leave the girl alone," said Ms. Weathersby. "I'm sorry Rose I should've told you. Now let's eat. Vince has prepared a wonderful dinner, and it's getting cold with all this chatter."

Patrice winked at Rose then asked her to pass the butter. Rose smiled, knowing full well why she winked. She hoped it was enough to earn her trust.

After dinner was over and the dishes washed, Vince came out to speak to Rose.

"Rose, can I talk to you for a minute?"

"Sure Vince, what's up?"

"I had to see you. I couldn't stop thinking about you."

"Why Mr. Hamlin, why would you be thinking 'bout little ole me?"

"I'm serious Rose, I really wanted to see you. Somehow, I thought, maybe, you were thinking of me?"

"Vince you know I just got out of prison. Why are you interested in me? You are a very attractive man. You can have any woman you want. Young, old and probably even rich."

"Money doesn't motivate me, Rose. It's the beauty inside as well as out, that attracts my attention."

He started reaching for her. She backed up.

"Take you, for instance, the way you wear your hair, your smile. The confidence you have in yourself. You're like a breath of fresh air around this place. I've never met anyone like you."

Vince started moving closer.

"I feel I can tell you anything. All of my adult life, I've prayed that God would one day send me a soul mate. He showed me you, Rose. You're my soul mate."

For the first time in her life, Rose was speechless. She backed up again.

"Vince, I don't know what to say."

Vince continued speaking while moving closer.

"I knew from the first time you said grace at dinner that you would be someone special in my life. I know this may be a bit too much, too fast for you to digest right now, Rose, just please give me a chance. I want to know you better. I want to know everything about you."

Rose placed her hand up to block him from coming closer.

"Oh no, you don't mister. I can't believe this. This is way too easy. You want to know me better? Please! Give me a break!"

Rose put her hand on her hip, then started walking around Vince as she spoke.

"A nobody who was raised in a whorehouse and just getting out of prison. Come on now Vince, who are you kidding, and who put you up to this? How do I know you're not playing with me? My grandmother taught me enough about men to know what they want."

Rose knew what she said hurt. Vince looked at her as if she had stabbed him in his heart. Without saying another word, he turned and walked down the hall to his room and closed the door.

Rose didn't see Ms. Weathersby standing in the doorway of the living room until she turned to go upstairs to her room. She wondered how much she heard.

"Sit down Rose. I have something I'd like to say to you."

Rose sat feeling like she was back in court. She didn't like it. She was sure she was going to get put out because of what just happened. According to Candy, Vince was off limits to all the girls at Farmington House.

"Rose, I couldn't help but hear the conversation between you and Vince. Eavesdropping is not something I make a habit of doing."

Rose cut in, "I'm sorry Ms. Weathersby it'll never happen again. I swear, I did nothing to urge him on like that."

"Rose, I see you have a lot to learn about men."

"What do you mean?" asked Rose

"Listen to me, dear. Never have I heard Vince pour his heart out to any woman as he has done to you." Why I might go as far to say I think he loves you.

"He can't love me, he just met me," Rose laughed. "He said I was his soul mate. I don't even know what that is."

"Rose women of all races wish they had a soul mate. Someone they could share all their hopes and dreams with, love, cherish and grow old with. A person like that only comes from God. Now he thinks you're his soul mate, and you have just torn his heart out. Now you'll have to go in there and fix it. I don't want him upset trying to cook for me."

Ms. Weathersby laughed after she made her speech, then started walking to her room.

"How do I fix it?" Rose called to Ms. Weathersby.

Ms. Weathersby stopped walking. "Just tell me one thing Rose then I'm done with this conversation. Do you want him?"

Rose was stunned with Ms. Weathersby's forwardness. She couldn't believe she knew so much about love and stuff.

"I'm waiting for your answer, Rose."

Rose answered jokingly. "Well, he is fine and has a killer body."

Ms. Weathersby quickly responded, "Rose, looks and a great body are a bonus in a relationship, but they fade. It has to be more than that, or this conversation was all in vain."

"I don't know if what I feel is love or not but, I get butterflies in my stomach when I just think about him, Rose confessed.

Rose grabbed her stomach. "Like now and I'm just talking about him. It's weird."

"Well, I guess weird will have to be enough for right now."

"Vince is very dear to me, Rose. I promised his mother on her death bed, I would take care of him. I really don't want to see him hurt. In all these years he's been here cooking his little heart out, he finally finds someone he's interested in, and you hurt him. Now go in there."

"Wait a minute, said Rose, I thought Candy's mother died giving birth to her here?"

"She did, and your point is?"

"Now you said Vince's mother died here too?"

"Yes, that's right. Vince's mom and dad came here from England when he was only eight. They were going to start a new life here. My guess is Vince's dad was disenchanted with America and went back to England. Except he took what little money they had and left them at the bus station.

"That's terrible," Rose said.

"That's where I found them, huddled in a blanket asleep and starving. They didn't know anyone, so I took them home with me. Vince hadn't heard from his father since. He likes to think of him as being dead. I guess that makes it easier for him to accept his father leaving them."

Rose added, "lucky for them you came along when you did. No telling what would have happened if you hadn't."

Ms. Weathersby stared into space as she continued with her story.

"Farmington House had just opened, to take in borders and we really needed a cook. Clara was going to do the cooking but thank God we didn't have to depend on that. Vince's mother Hannah turned out to be an excellent cook. She cooked at Farmington for many years before she got ill and died. She taught Vince most of everything he knows about cooking. Except for what he learned in culinary school. He enjoys it. But it doesn't take the place of a mate."

"I'm so sorry, I didn't know," said Rose feeling a little sad.

"I know you didn't mean to hurt him Rose and I also know you've been down a rough road yourself. Now stop your talking and get in there."

Chapter 19

Rose walked slowly to Vince's room. Her heartbeat was the only sound she could hear.

"I can't believe I'm doing this, she said to herself. God, I hope I'm doing the right thing. If he doesn't answer when I knock the first time, I'm leaving this alone."

Rose knocked lightly on the door hoping Vince would not hear, so she wouldn't have to go in.

"Yes, who's there?"

She gritted her teeth then spoke. "It's me, Rose, may I come in?"

"I don't feel like another stab in my heart, Rose," Vince said coldly.

"Vince please, I have something to say, may I come in?"

Rose shut her eyes, then leaned her head against the door.

"If you must, the door is not locked."

Rose entered the room slowly, then closed the door. The fragrance from a eucalyptus plant sitting on the nightstand filled the air. The lights were dimmed. Rose looked around the room and noticed how neat everything was. Vince sat on the side of the bed with his shirt off, and his hair dangling in his face. He sat in silence, not bothering to look up with his hands clasped together. This time Rose saw his whole chest and all she could think of was how gorgeous he was.

"Stay focused, Rose," she told herself.

Rose went over to the side of the bed where Vince sat then kneeled down in front of him. With her heart still pounding, she raised his head and moved his hair out of his face. Rose looked in his eyes, staring deeply; as if she could see into his soul. She couldn't help but, see the hurt she caused. She wished she could have taken back what she said. The longer she stared into his eyes, the more she knew he really meant what he said.

"Fix it," was all she could hear Ms. Weathersby saying in her mind. How could I? He won't even talk to me, she thought.

Vince tried turning his face away from her but, she wouldn't let him. She held his face and without saying a word, kissed him. He backed up as if she had shocked him.

"I'm sorry," she said, "I didn't know what else to do."

He rose off the bed, lifting her up with him. He placed his hands now on her face and, returned her kiss.

Rose began talking nervously. "Vince, I'm sorry I hurt you, I didn't mean half the things I said. I was afraid. I don't want to get hurt. Most of the women I knew in prison were put there by a man one way or another."

Vince placed his finger to her lips. "I'll never hurt you, Rose, I promise." He kissed her again. Rose realized she felt more for him than she was willing to admit. She turned to leave. He grabbed her arm.

"I must go," she said. "I should not be here."

He smiled, "If you must go, know this, I love you."

Rose stood in her tracks, paralyzed.

"You love me? Vince, we hardly know each other. How do you know if what you feel for me isn't lust?"

Vince turned serious, "my heart knows the difference between love and lust Rose."

"I'm sorry, Vince. I didn't mean that the way it sounded."

"Rose is my loving you so hard for you to believe. I have no reason to lie or look further. You are the one for me, and someday very soon I'll prove it."

Rose couldn't believe what she heard him say. It was like a dream, and she didn't want anyone to wake her.

"Rose, did you hear what I said?"

Rose snapped out of her little dreamland and answered. "Yes, Vince, I heard you. I just don't believe what I'm hearing."

He kissed her once more. "Believe it."

Rose broke out of his embrace. "I better go."

Vince pulled her in his arms once again. Holding her close, he whispered, "stay with me tonight, Rose."

Rose broke away again. "I can't. What about Ms. Weathersby and the others? I just can't."

"I'm sorry, I understand." He leaned in closer to her. "Let me walk you to your room?"

Rose laughed, putting both hands on his chest to stop him from coming closer.

"No need Mr. Hamlin, I can't handle any more of your charm tonight."

Vince lifted her chin and kissed her again.

"Sweet dreams," he said.

Rose left Vince's room and hurried back to hers. She fell against the door when she got inside, she let out a deep breath. She looked in the mirror then checked her hair.

She spoke to her reflection. "Rose, you are in big trouble. Sweet dreams, he said. I won't be able to sleep at all."

She checked her face for any imperfections, "God, I wish Bea was here. I need some help."

She changed into her night clothes and went to bed.

Chapter 20

Rose awoke Sunday morning, her head spinning with the thoughts of last night. Realizing the time, she jumped out of bed.

"Oh no! I'm going to be late for my first day at church. Why didn't someone wake me?"

Rose fussed around her room, trying to find something to wear. Holding up two dresses, she decided to wear the dress Candy had given her when she first arrived.

"God I really miss my clothes," she said, as she threw the dress on the bed, and ran in the washroom down the hall.

She noticed the quiet. Quickly jumped in and out of the shower, brushed her teeth, and rushed back to her room. She tried hard to keep her mind off Vince.

She told herself, "stop it, Rose, you cannot let this man take over your thoughts."

Rose grabbed a large hair clip, twisted her locks into a bun, clamped on the clip. She grabbed her shoes and raced downstairs to find no one eating breakfast. She looked in the kitchen, Vince wasn't there either. She wondered where everyone was. There was one plate covered on the stove that had her name on it.

She grabbed the plate, said grace then hurriedly ate.

"Thank you, Vince, I must have done something right to have a man like that like me."

She walked to the nearest church. It was small. It had a steeple and a huge cross on the roof. It was painted, three different colors. The body was white, the windows and doors were green, and the stairs leading up to the entrance were yellow. She noticed the name. True Believers Missionary Baptist Church. Rev. Eugene Clayton, Pastor.

Rose giggled to herself while walking up the stairs. "Well, hello True Believers, here comes Rose Hill."

She attempted to pull open the doors. The usher gave her a signal not to enter. She waited on the steps. After devotion was over, they allowed her to come in. Rose felt relieved she wasn't the only one coming in late. She looked around for a place to sit. To her surprise, Ms. Weathersby, Vince, and Candy were already seated. Ms. Weathersby waved for her to come over and sit next to her.

Rose whispered to Ms. Weathersby, "why didn't you tell me you guys went to this church?" I've been looking for a place to go. I only chose this one because it was the closest to Farmington House."

Ms. Weathersby responded, "I'm glad you came. Now pipe down the Pastors coming out."

The choir had just finished singing. Pastor Clayton stepped out onto the pulpit. Rose sat at attention, watching every move he made. He's exactly what I imagined a pastor would look like Salt and pepper hair, mustache, even his build. He sort of resembles Warden Powell.

Pastor Clayton's voice rising high, then low, broke her thoughts. She noticed how he emphasized every other word he said. Rose marveled at how different the service was compared to the service in the joint. She listened intently to the message but did not notice Vince trying to get her attention until Candy called her name. She finally turned around to say hello, then was shushed by an older woman in the next pew. Vince smiled, then winked at her.

When service was over, Ms. Weathersby pulled Rose to the side.

"Rose, I don't know what you said to Vince last night, but it worked. He's been cheesing all morning. You two didn't do anything last night you'll be sorry about later, did you?"

Rose was shocked by her question, trying not to appear guilty.

Mrs. Weathersby didn't wait for her to answer this time. She shook her head as if she was erasing the idea from her mind.

"Anyhow, I'll see you back at the house. I've got to get out of these shoes. I paid too much money for my feet to hurt. These babies will be going back to the store."

Ms. Weathersby limped out of the church. She shook the Pastors hand then walked down the stairs. Candy lingered behind.

"Candy, come on girl, my feet are killing me. The least you could do is help me down the street."

"Coming, yelled Candy," running down the stairs to catch her.

"Mum, why did you buy them shoes anyway. I told you they looked like they would hurt your feet before you bought them."

"Oh, mind your business girl and give me your arm. You're going to find out one day, that all ladies dress shoes hurt your feet. Men design 'em and women buy 'em. Keep on living, you're going to be buying them too."

Candy mumbled. "Not if I can help it."

Rose stayed behind to shake Pastors Clayton's hand. She introduced herself.

"Hi, I'm Rose. I enjoyed your sermon. I've never heard the word preached with so much emotion before."

"Why thank you, Rose, it was not me, but the spirit of God within me that delivered the message. I see this is your first time here at True Believers."

"Yes, it is," said Rose.

"Well, don't leave without filling out a visitor's card. Hope to see you next Sunday, or even on Wednesday night for Bible class."

"I'd love to come," said Rose.

Rose felt a sense of peace shaking his hand. She smiled.

"Include me in your prayers, Pastor?"

"Indeed, I will, Rose."

She rushed out trying to catch up with the others when Vince stopped her at the top of the stairs.

"Looking for me," Vince said smoothly.

He grabbed her hand and escorted her down the stairs.

"You didn't think I would just leave without you, did you, Rose?"

She smiled, "I'm glad you didn't."

They walked slowly back to the house. Two women who looked to be in their twenties walked up behind them.

The younger of the two spoke first. "Vince you could have said you were leaving so soon."

Rose let go of Vince's hand.

The other spoke, "Yes, Vincent, you have always walked us home from church, what happened?"

The two women looked Rose up and down then turned to Vince.

The younger one asked, "who is your friend?"

Vince turned to Rose then grabbed her hand again.

"Ladies, this is Miss Rose Hill she's new at Farmington House."

The older of the two stated, "Farmington House, then that makes you an ex." She stopped speaking in mid-sentence and grabbed the younger girl's arm.

"Come Georgia we better go!"

"Talk to you later, Vince!" yelled Georgia snickering.

Curious Rose asked. "Vince, who were they?"

"That was Carmen and her little sister Georgia. They're Pastor Clayton's nieces."

Rose said, sounding disappointed, "you would have thought I had a disease the way she rushed off."

"Never mind them, Rose, you're with me now," said Vince.

Rose grabbed Vince's arm as they continued their walk to the house. Thinking, so this is how they treat ex-cons. I guess I shouldn't be surprised. Rose snapped out of her daydream hoping Vince didn't notice it bothered her.

"Vince, I need to mail a letter to my mother. Where's the nearest mailbox?"

Vince held Rose by the waist. "A letter to mommy, eh? Did you tell her all about me?"

"Aren't you, Mr. Confident. If you must know, I didn't mention you at all." Rose smirked.

Vince looked at her surprised. Rose bumped him with her hips.

"Don't worry yourself. I told them all about you."

"Them?" asked Vince.

"Oh yes, I have many friends in the joint." I'm sure they'd like you.

"They sound like nice people." Vince smiled.

"All except Big Bertha, she might want to hurt you."

Rose laughed then became saddened. Vince noticed her mood change.

He asked, "Is something wrong Rose?"

"I don't know if I'll ever see my mother again. They won't let an ex-con visit another while in prison."

Vince took Rose's hand. "I'm sorry Rose maybe one day you'll be able to see her again."

He tried changing the subject, "there's your mailbox." He pointed across the street.

"Give me the letter. I'll drop it in the box for you."

Rose watched as Vince ran across the street dodging traffic. It made her feel special to know he cared so much about her. She thought to herself again, Grandma Jessie would have loved you too.

They talked all the way back to the house. They stopped on the porch then sat down.

"Now you know my story, Vince. I hope you understand why I'm the way I am?"

"You're perfect Rose, as far as I'm concerned."

"You always know the right things to say, Vince. Rose smiled, then kissed him on the cheek.

"Rose, I know I should go in and start dinner. I hate to leave you, especially now that we're learning so much about each other. We both lost people we loved dearly. I wish I had known your grandmother and I wish you could have known my mother."

"So do I Vince."

Vince went inside to find Candy, Violet, and Stacey at the window, pretending not to have been eavesdropping.

He laughed. "Beautiful day isn't it ladies?"

They each bolted out onto the porch to talk to Rose.

Candy yelled first, "I knew it! He's got the hots for you, Rose!"

Stacey asked, "How did you do it? Patrice has been trying to get Vince to like her for a long time now. Just wait until she finds out."

"She's gonna be really mad at you, Rose," said Violet.

Rose looked from one girl to the other. This time she felt no need to defend herself.

"Patrice is the least of my worries right now. If anything, she'll need to worry about me," Rose said coyly.

Not understanding what Rose meant, all at once, Candy, Stacey, and Violet started laughing.

Candy began teasing Rose. "Rose got a boyfriend! Rose got a boyfriend!"

"How juvenile," commented Rose.

Ms. Weathersby rushed out, "what's all the noise about?"

Violet and Stacey rushed inside, leaving Candy and Rose to fend for themselves. Candy ran past Ms. Weathersby almost knocking her over.

Ms. Weathersby yelled. "Candy! Slow down, girl!"

"Sorry!" Candy yelled back, laughing, running up the stairs.

Rose giggled. "Thank you for helping me with Vince, Ms. Weathersby. It turns out he's a real gentleman."

"You're welcome dear, said Ms. Weathersby still puzzled over Candy's action.

Rose started inside.

"Rose, please stay awhile?"

Ms. Weathersby sat on the porch swing. Come have a seat."

She patted on the swing's cushion next to her.

Rose walked over slowly, then sat down.

"You know Rose, there is something about you that makes me feel especially closer to you than the other girls. I don't know what it is, but I'm glad you're here. Feel free to talk to me anytime you like. You'll find I'm a pretty good listener too."

"I'll remember that," Rose said. "I'm going to go up to my room now to get ready for tomorrow."

Rose went into her room. The term having the bitter with the sweet came to mind. She knew she couldn't tell anyone what was going on at the nursing home and she couldn't continue to stay at Farmington House, not with Vince just down the hall. She wanted him as much as he wanted her. The temptation was great for both of them. Just thinking of it all made her feel tired. She laid down for a nap and fell asleep.

Chapter 21

After Sis. Mona received Rose's letter she read it to the entire Bible study class. Everyone was happy to hear from her. They all had many questions. Sis. Mona agreed to allow them to write a letter in class and she would send it out.

Big Bertha spoke up first. "Ask her to send me a picture of Vince."

All the ladies agreed about the picture.

Bea asked. "Why would she send you a picture of Vince?"

"I'm asking for all of us. I just want to see what the guy that stole Rose's heart looks like. You know, that girl was not easy to get along with especially when she first got here."

The ladies shook their heads in agreement once again.

Bea exclaimed. "Now, get off my Rose!

Bertha added, "Bea, you know yourself what a hot head that girl had when she first got here."

"What I do know is, you all better leave my Rose alone. I'm glad she found someone. And, I better not hear tell of him hurting a hair on her head, or me and Bertha will bust out of here, and break his neck."

Bertha laughed. "What makes you think I'm gonna bust out with you Bea?"

Bea laughed also. "You don't think I'm gonna do it by myself do you?"

Sis. Mona spoke up, no need to plan a prison break ladies, she will be fine.

"You're right Sis. Mona, 'cause I taught Rose just what to do if a joker tried something." Bertha demonstrated a kick to the groin then winked at Bea.

"I don't want to know what that was Bertha, we'll just keep Rose in our prayers," said Sis. Mona.

Most of the Bible study hour was used compiling a letter to, Rose. Everyone got a chance to ask a question or two. Sis. Mona added what she wanted and then asked everyone to pray especially hard for Rose now that she was on the outside.

Back in her cell, Bea pulled out the old photos of Rose and her mother, Jessie. She smiled and wept at the same time. Her heart ached from missing them so. At that moment Thelma one of the guards approached Bea's cell.

"It's time Bea."

Bea, raised her head, wiped her eyes, and asked, "it's time, time for what?"

Thelma answered. "Come on now Bea, you know every year the review board hears your case and discusses it with you."

"I forgot that was today. I don't know why they even bother, it's the same thing every year with the same old stupid questions. How are you, Bea? How have you been getting along Bea? Are you sorry for what you did Bea? If you should be paroled, what will you do? Like they're going to parole me. They deny me every year. Why do I have to keep going? It's just a waste of time."

Bea stood still waiting for Thelma to answer. Thelma reached to grab Bea's arm.

"Time is all you have in here Bea. You go through this every year. Just come on before they start looking for the both of us."

Bea entered the meeting room then looked around for the familiar faces she sees every year. This time to her surprise, Warden Powell was there.

"Hello Warden, what are you doing here?" Bea asked.

"Hello Bea, I'm here for a special reason this time, but first, I'll let the review board's secretary Miss Brown have the floor."

"Alright," said Bea looking puzzled as she took her seat.

Miss Brown put on her glasses and began reading.

"In the case of The State of Massachusetts vs. Bea Harris, it has been found herewith, by the State of Massachusetts Chief Justice Herman Masters, that the punishment for the said criminal act by defendant Bea Harris, has been deemed as time served, and she shall be released from the MCI Framingham Correctional Center for Women, no sooner than June 5, 2002, and no later than June 30, 2002."

Miss Brown slowly removed her glasses and sat down. Bea stared at her, not believing what she had just heard.

Warden Powell asked, "Bea, did you understand what Miss Brown just read?"

"If I'm not mistaken Warden, it sounded like she said I'm going to be released from prison, but I know that can't be right."

"It is right Bea," said Warden Powell. "It was found that your punishment did not fit your crime. Although you killed your husband, they know now after reviewing your case more, that you killed him in self-defense. It seems somebody up there has been looking out for you. You will be released in one week, as soon as we find somewhere to place you. Now mind you, you will have to report to a parole officer."

Bea stood up from her seat then fell back down to the floor onto her knees. She didn't care who watched her.

"It's a miracle!" she cried. "Thank, You God!"

Miss Brown smiled, pulled a hanky from her purse then wiped a tear from her eye. Warden Powell asked the guard to come in and take Bea back to her cell. Bea could hardly stand without help. She cried and laughed all at the same time.

"Did you hear the news Thelma? I'm going home."

Thelma stood sternly trying not to show any emotion.

"Yes, I did Bea, and I'm happy for you."

Bea grabbed her from the side and gave her a hug. Thelma broke free of Bea's hug, looked around quickly to see who was watching.

"Don't be getting all mushy on me Bea, people will start to talk."

"Oh, hush Thelma, I'm going to miss you too."

Thelma cleared her throat. "Come on now Bea before you make cry. I don't want the other women around here to see me bawling like a baby. I got a reputation to uphold in this place."

The other ladies wondered what the commotion was about when Bea got back to her cell. Big Bertha started consoling Bea right away when she saw her.

"Sorry Bea, you'll get'em next time."

Bea looked at Bertha then began speaking very slowly.

"No need to be sorry Bertha, I'm going home to my Rose."

Big Bertha asked, "what you talkin 'bout Bea, you going home to your Rose?"

Bea repeated herself again. "Bertha, I'm going home. They're letting me go after twenty-four years in this place, they are letting me go."

Bertha stared at Bea, then shouted, "Bea's going home everybody! Bea's going home!"

Bea laughed, "calm down Bertha before they put you in solitaire."

Bertha asked, now being more serious, "Bea, how is it possible they're letting you out?"

Bea explained the best she could. She sat down on her bunk with Bertha at her side.

"Bert, as I understand it, they said, the punishment did not fit the crime, so I've served enough time, and now I can go home. Where ever that is, as long as it's away from here."

Bertha exclaimed, "you're in here for murder just like me. You think they'll let me out too?"

"I wouldn't know about that Bertha but, what I do know is, with God, anything's possible. I never thought I'd see Rose again so soon, but I am. So never stop praying and believing."

Bea rushed out of her cell.

"I'll see you later, Bertha. I've got to stop Sis. Mona from mailing that letter to Rose. I've got to tell her the good news."

Sis. Mona had just waved goodbye to the mail carrier when Bea came running up.

"Wait!" Bea yelled.

The mail truck pulled out of the yard. Bea let out a sigh of disappointment.

Out of breath, she complained. "Oh crap, now I'll have to wait till tomorrow."

Sis. Mona called out. "Bea, what's wrong?"

Bea leaned on the wall trying to catch her breath.

"It's not what's wrong Mona it's what's right.

She took a deep breath and began to speak.

"Mona, they're letting me go home. I wanted to stop that letter from going out, so I could tell Rose right away."

"Bea that's wonderful news. Why didn't they tell me?"

I don't know why they didn't tell you Mona. Maybe the Warden knows, you and I are pretty close friends, and he didn't want you spoiling the surprise for me.

Sis Mona gave Bea a hug. "If anyone deserves this Bea it's you."

"You know what that means Mona? I'm going to see Rose again."

"You see Bea," said Sis. Mona. "God rewards those who are faithful. Don't worry about telling Rose. We can write to her first thing tomorrow."

"Well, I guess I can wait another day, I've waited over twenty years."

Sis. Mona gave Bea another hug while holding back her tears.

"Bea, out of all the students I've had, you have become a true friend of mine. I'm going to miss you. First Rose and now you."

Sis. Mona pulled out a handkerchief from her sleeve, then blew her nose. "Don't ever lose that thirst you have for the word. I'm so proud of you."

Chapter 22

Monday morning, it was just like Rose thought. Patrice had nothing to say about hers, and Vince's relationship. She didn't like it, but she dared not say anything, fearing Rose might let on about the casino. Rose was just about to leave for work when Patrice came up.

"Wait, Rose, I'll walk with you to work."

Rose figured this would be her chance to get any information she could, to help Linda with the investigation.

"I know you need money. I can help you with that if you want?"

Rose pretended not to know what she meant. "I'll be alright once I earn my first paycheck."

Patrice laughed, "girl I'm not talking about the few pennies Mrs. Wilson will be paying you. I'm talking about more money you will ever see working in a nursing home."

Rose stopped walking, then turned to Patrice. "Alright you got my attention, now tell me more."

Patrice whispered, "I'll do better than tell you, I'll show you".

When they arrived at the Nursing Home, Patrice took Rose to a back entrance that was covered by a huge billboard. Once inside, Patrice entered into another door that read emergency exit only. They went down a flight of stairs that led to another door. Patrice knocked twice.

Bo asked, disguising his voice. "What's the password?"

Rose almost laughed when she heard Patrice recite the password through the door.

"Step on a crack, break your mama's back."

"I wonder what genius thought that up?" mumbled Rose.

Bo opened the door. To his surprise, Rose was standing there. He smiled at first then he turned serious. "Patrice, what's she doing here?"

Pushing her way in pass Bo, Patrice responded. "Oh, she's alright. She wants a piece of the action. She could have blown our cover back at the house, but she didn't, in my book that makes her alright. Who's watching the door upstairs?"

"Mr. Culpepper is the lookout this time. He's pretending to do the books again," said Bo.

Patrice asked, "Where's that nosey nurse Linda? She's always snooping around."

Rose butted in trying to take the suspicion off Linda.

"Well, she does work here, Patrice."

"Work here or not, if she keeps it up, she's going to be sorry. She's been here a few months, and everywhere I turn there she is."

Rose couldn't believe what she saw. It was just like Linda said. They had everything they needed to run a casino. Roulette wheel, slot machines, blackjack table, even dealers. It was amazing, she thought to herself, this guy Culpepper really does have a lot of nerve. To think he did all this right under everyone's noses. Well, won't he be surprised when he gets busted?

Rose asked, still looking around, "How did you hook up with Mr. Culpepper? And how did he get everything inside?"

Patrice answered, "If you must know miss nosey, Culpepper and I go way back. I did a few years in the state penitentiary covering his butt. He knows he owes me big time. I turned him on to Mrs. Wilson place. It was easy getting everything in with her being blind and all. I hate this is happening to the old girl, but I need money. I can't stand living at Farmington House."

Rose stood stoned faced trying not to let her feelings show through. She couldn't help thinking, God don't like ugly. Your fun is coming to an end real soon.

Patrice continued bragging. "You see Rose, Culpepper and I have a really good understanding if you know what I mean. I make him believe he could have this at any time."

Patrice ran her hands up and down her body as if she was strumming a guitar. Rose watched as Patrice went on with her display of self worship.

"Understand now, I've never let him taste the fruit you know. I just make him lots of promises that one day he will. He believes it too, the poor fool."

Patrice let out an evil laugh. Rose pretending what she said was funny, laughed with her.

"Tell me, girl, what do I want with a Mr. Peabody look alike? Hell, he can't handle this no way. As soon as I get enough money, I am off to Las Vegas, Nevada."

Rose finally cut in. "Patrice what would you do if you don't make enough money?"

"Well, I'll just have to go to Plan B."

"Plan B, what's plan B?"

"Oh, No! Miss Thing, I can't tell you all my secrets, that's between me and my maker."

"Speaking of your maker Patrice, why didn't I see you in church Sunday?"

"Church? Girl please, I don't go to nobody's church. We do our best business on Sunday, and believe you me, the closest I'll come to church is standing next to some of those church folks that come up in here."

Patrice gave out another laugh. This time Rose didn't think what she said was funny at all. She remembered how she reacted when Bea tried to tell her about church. Rose wondered if she sounded as bad as Patrice did.

Patrice took Rose to meet Mr. Culpepper. Rose looked him up and down. It was just like Patrice said, she thought. He was the spitting image of that little dog with glasses. Mr. Culpepper looked down his glasses at Rose then asked, "how long you been out?"

Rose frowned, and then answered, "only a few days."

"Well if you don't want to go back, you'll keep your mouth shut and your eyes open. If you can do that, we'll all make a lot of money in a short time. I'm not in this for the long haul. I've got things to do, and people to do it too." He winked at Patrice, then told Rose, "you're on lookout for now."

Instantly, Rose knew she didn't like Culpepper, she also knew she couldn't let on about it. She thought to herself, good thing he put me on lookout. I'll be able to talk to Linda easily.

Rose asked, "how can I be the look out, and work as a Nurses' Aide too?"

"Easy," said Patrice, "just work only on this floor and stop anyone that tries to come in this door."

"What if I'm assigned to another floor?"

Patrice answered, "Oh, don't worry about that honey I'm in charge of scheduling the assignments. Sweet, ain't it?"

Patrice nudged Culpepper then laughed. Rose was about to ask another what if question when Culpepper cut her off.

"Save your questions for Jeopardy sweet pea, we're losing money standing here, we've got customers waiting."

Rose frowned. Then stood in front of the door. "I'll be your sweet pea right now but your days are numbered too, she said with her back against the door."

Chapter 23

Bea waited anxiously for the mail to go out. She wished she could be there when Rose read she would be getting out. Maybe it's better this way she thought, once she gets the first letter, she won't expect a second to come so soon.

Rose was on her third day of being the lookout man. She was able to talk to Linda anytime she liked.

"They've made it so easy, Rose, putting you on lookout. My Captain is really grateful for all your help. He wants to meet you when this is over."

Linda checked for her revolver.

"Well, Rose it's almost time. I have everyone in place and ready to go. Just wait for my signal."

Rose asked nervously, "signal, what signal?"

Linda whispered, "you'll know, just get down low and stay there until it's over."

Rose started talking to herself, "Oh my god, I guess this is it. I'm so nervous. Mrs. Wilson doesn't deserve this."

Rose yelled, "Linda! Mrs. Wilson doesn't know this is about to happen, she'll be scared to death."

Rose started down the hall when she heard Linda call out.

"Rose! Where are you going?"

Rose walked at a fast pace. "I'm going to get Mrs. Wilson out of here! She's alone!"

"Rose don't!" yelled Linda down the hall. "Things have to look as normal as possible, she'll be alright!"

Rose returned and stood by the lab door, wringing her hands nervously. She watched Linda's every move.

Linda casually walked up to her. "Rose, stay calm, it's almost over."

Patrice and Mr. Culpepper came in at the same time. Rose stood up straight.

Patrice spoke to Linda. "Hey Linda, how's it going?"

Linda spoke, trying to be as cheerful as possible. "Hello, Patrice; good day, Mr. Culpepper."

Patrice walked over to Rose. "Has the snoop sister been a problem?"

Rose answered as calmly as she could. "No, she's been cool."

Rose noticed Culpepper talk to Linda at the nurse's station. That was his usual method of distraction, to keep Linda from noticing Patrice sneaking in the Lab door. Lame, Rose thought to herself, he is so lame. It was now her turn to create a diversion for Culpepper to sneak in the lab.

"Linda!" Rose called out. "I can't seem to get the measurements right on this prescription for Mr. Brown's insulin. Can you help me? I don't want to make any mistakes."

Linda excused herself from talking to Mr. Culpepper. "I'll show you how Rose. You're right we don't want any mistakes."

Culpepper slipped in the lab as soon as Linda turned her back.

After waiting a minute or two, Linda whistled loudly, with her two fingers up to her lips. Seconds after that, in rushed cop, after cop, each one carrying weapons and wearing bulletproof vests. Linda reached under her dress, then unstrapped from her leg, her own weapon. Rose fell to the floor as they kicked in the lab door. Some went in, some stayed out. Linda rushed in right along with the rest.

Rose saw Mrs. Wilson coming down the hall using the railing as her guide.

She called out, "What's all the noise out here?"

Rose ran up to her and pulled her down to the floor. "Don't worry Mrs. Wilson, it's me, Rose. I'm here with you, there are cops all over the place."

"Cops? Why are the police here? What's happened?"

"Stay down, Mrs. Wilson! You don't want to get hurt!"

Rose held on to Mrs. Wilson tightly. She was afraid to let go; afraid something would happen to her. The screaming, the cries, the noise, all too many familiar sounds that brought back her nightmare of when she was arrested, and when her grandmother died in her arms. She began to cry uncontrollably, holding her ears.

Mrs. Wilson felt for Roses' face, then put her arms around her, she started rocking, back and forth, "there, there, my child, it's alright, it's alright I'm here."

At that very moment, Rose felt as if her Grandma Jessie was there. A sense of calm came over her.

She looked up at Mrs. Wilson. "Grandma? Grandma Jessie?"

"No dear, I'm not your grandma. It's me, Mrs. Wilson. Are you alright?"

Rose wiped her face and then sat up. "Oh, I'm sorry, Mrs. Wilson, for a moment there you sound like my grandmother. I feel better now. I'll explain later why the police are here."

The cops began bringing people out. Rose didn't realize how many people were in the small room. Linda kept her promise she brought Bo out in cuffs first. After Bo, an officer brought out Patrice, kicking and screaming. Patrice looked down the hall and saw Rose and called to her. "Rose! You were in on this the whole time? You dirty b__!" The officer grabbed her mouth and escorted her outside.

Mrs. Wilson asked, "is that Patrice I here? Was she a part of this mess?"

"I'm afraid so Mrs. Wilson, but she wasn't the only one. Bo and Mr. Culpepper were in on it too."

Saddened Mrs. Wilson replied. "Oh, not Bo. In on what? He was such a nice young man, and a hard worker too."

Rose spoke slowly, "Mrs. Wilson, Mr. Culpepper ran a gambling casino in the old lab that was not in use anymore."

"You mean the accountant, that did my books? He did all this without me knowing?"

"Yes, it seems that man has cheated a lot of people out of a lot of money over the years, and they've been after him for a long time."

Rose helped Mrs. Wilson up from the floor. "Come, Mrs. Wilson, I'll tell you how I became involved in this. When I started here, Linda asked me if I could help her and the police, bust them. I never thought it would be like this."

"You said, Linda? I don't have a nurse working here by the name Linda."

"I'm sorry Mrs. Wilson there has been a lot of deception around you. Linda is not really a nurse she's a cop, working undercover here to catch Mr. Culpepper. I didn't know any of this until I got here. I helped the cops get the information they needed to bust them. I didn't have a choice."

At last, they brought Mr. Culpepper out. Rose thought, she would be pleased to see him get arrested but, it only sickened her.

"Thank God it's over," said Rose.

Thank God is right Rose. "I'm the one to blame for all of this. I should have had a background check done on Mr. Culpepper when

Patrice told me about him. He said he knew my husband. I guess that was a lie too. My books were in shambles. I just wanted someone to straighten them out."

Mrs. Wilson wiped the tears from her eyes. "This never would have happened if I were able to see."

Don't beat yourself up, Mrs. Wilson. "Some people are just naturally not nice. It's not your fault, said, Rose.

Linda came back inside and saw them both still clinging to each other.

"You two can relax now! It's over! I'd like to thank you personally, Rose, for helping us. Don't worry about Patrice she'll be away for a little while. You did the right thing."

Chapter 24

The news of the Nursing Home Casino bust was all over town. Mrs. Weathersby, Vince, and even Clara bombarded Rose with questions concerning what happened.

Ms. Weathersby asked first, "Rose, why didn't you tell us, what was going on?"

"I couldn't tell anyone, Ms. Weathersby it was an ongoing investigation. I was recruited to help them the very first day I started."

"You could have told me, Rose," said Vince.

"No, I couldn't Vince. It wasn't my decision. I had no choice."

Vince walked over and gave Rose a hug. "I'm just glad you were not harmed."

Stacey and Violet looked at each other and giggled.

Candy shouted, "this is the most excitement we've had in a long time! I can't wait to go back to school, I'll be like a celebrity!"

Ms. Weathersby scolded, "Candy! This isn't anything to be excited about. Rose could have been hurt, and Patrice was arrested. Lord knows how Mrs. Wilson is taking this."

"Poor Patrice said Stacey, I'll miss her."

"Well, I won't," said Violet. "She was too bossy."

"Shame on you, Violet," said Ms. Weathersby, "that child can surely use your prayers now. Never kick a man when he's down."

Violet looked at Stacey, then muttered under her breath, "I didn't kick anybody, she did that to herself."

Candy looked up at the ceiling, "okay now, I'm getting bored. I'm out of here."

Candy was on her way upstairs when she heard the mailman drop the mail through the slot. "I'll get it!"

She hurriedly sorted through the mail then yelled out, "Rose, here's one for you!"

Rose jumped up and grabbed the letter from Candy's hand.

"It's from Sis. Mona! I can't wait to hear how my mom and the others are doing. She can't write to me herself they won't allow it."

Rose opened the letter and then started reading it out loud. She laughed at their questions but skipped over the ones that gave reference to Vince. The more she read, the sadder she became.

Ms. Weathersby noticed the sadness in her voice. "Rose, you can read your letter later if you'd like."

Rose looked up from her letter and answered, "oh I'm alright."

Violet asked, "would you like me to read it for you, Rose?"

"No Violet, I can read it."

Ms. Weathersby tried to help Rose once again. "Tell me, Rose how is Mrs. Wilson doing after everything that's happened? I tried calling the Nursing Home to speak with her, but no one answered."

"I was able to talk to Mrs. Wilson last night she's at her daughters."

Ms. Weathersby cut in, "I didn't know she had a daughter."

"Yes, she does," continued Rose, "she's very nice."

It turns out; Mrs. Wilson has decided to sale the nursing home to the city and retire. They would have shut it down long before now if it wasn't for the investigation, because of the condition it was in. They're in the process of moving the residents to other facilities right away. She's finally going to stay home and enjoy her grandchildren. She's happy, and I'm happy for her too."

Well good for her, said Clara. "It was unnatural for her to be trying to run that place alone anyway."

Rose continued reading her letter, trying desperately not to show any emotion. The more she read, the more she missed Bea, Bertha, and all the others. She couldn't stand reading anymore, so she folded it up, excused herself, and went upstairs.

Vince looked at Ms. Weathersby. She nodded, giving him permission to go after her.

Vince could hear Rose crying in her room. He knocked on her door.

"Go away, Candy," she said.

He opened the door. "I'm sorry Rose, it's not Candy."

Rose sat up on the bed and straightened her clothes. "Vince it's you?"

"Yes, Rose. I could see reading your letter from your mom was making you sad, so I had to come up to see if you were alright."

"Oh, I'm alright, Vince. I just miss my mom so much, and it just breaks my heart to know I won't ever see her again.

Rose turned to the bedroom window and began to cry again. Vince stood next to her, then put his arms around her.

"Cry on me if you'd like my little butter toffee."

Rose stopped crying and started to laugh. "Butter toffee, I've never been compared to candy before."

Vince pulled a tissue from the tissue box on Rose's nightstand.

"You remind me of butter toffee, you're soft," he gently wiped the tears from her eyes, "you're sweet," he kissed her cheeks, and you're irresistible, he then kissed her lips."

"Umm," moaned Rose, "I'll never eat butter toffee the same again."

Rose jumped and backed away from him. "Whoa cowboy! You'll have to leave now, Mr. Hamlin. You should not be here."

Vince smiled a sheepish grin then walked over to her again.

"Mum knows I'm here, she sent me up to see about you."

"What about the others?" Rose asked. "What will they say?"

"Rose, I believe everyone in this house knows how I feel about you. It's no secret."

"Vince, I can't handle this now," Rose said nervously.

"Handle what?" I love you. You love me?"

With every word, he moved closer until Rose had no space between them.

"You do love me, don't you, Rose?" He stared her straight in her eyes, waiting for her to answer.

"I, I don't know," she answered, looking around her room, trying not to make eye contact.

Rose thought to herself. "Get it together girl, you can handle this, don't let him see you sweat. Don't let him know those baby brown eyes are driving you crazy."

Vince cupped Rose's face in his hands and kissed her again.

"Are you sure you don't know?" he asked.

"You're not playing fair, Mr. Hamlin." Rose's voice trembled as she spoke. You're trying to take advantage of me." God help me she murmured, as Vince continued kissing her softly, caressing her buttocks. Rose felt helpless. She knew she should stop him, but, her body didn't want him to stop. Her mind said no, but nothing came from her lips. She savored every touch, every kiss. She allowed him to touch her in places no man had ever touched before. She held him tight, running her hands through his hair, down his back. Feeling his man-ness grow larger and larger against her, she let out one more cry for help.

"God help me," she whispered.

At that very moment, there was a knock at the door.

"Rose! Vincent! It's me, may I come in?"

Vince and Rose both jumped at the same time. She broke away.

Trying to compose herself, she answered. "Yes, Ms. Weathersby come in." Vince immediately sat in a chair next to the bed, looking as cool as a cucumber. Rose was a wreck. She hoped Ms. Weathersby wouldn't suspect anything. Her mind was filled with guilt.

Ms. Weathersby sat on the bed then asked, "Rose, are you alright?"

Vince spoke quickly. "I'll go start dinner and let you ladies talk."

He looked at Rose, she looked away. He walked over to her, grabbed her chin, and kissed her again.

Ms. Weathersby hit him on his backside. "Go on Vincent leave the girl alone."

Rose wanted to shrink from embarrassment. She was speechless.

Ms. Weathersby started the conversation touching Rose's hand.

"Rose, I wondered what was taking Vincent so long to come back down. I thought I'd better come up and check on you myself. Is everything okay with your mother? You ran upstairs so quickly."

Rose spoke without looking at her, "yes, she's well, everyone is, I just miss her."

Ms. Weathersby lifted Rose's chin to see her face. "Something else is bothering you isn't it Rose?"

Rose confessed, looking down at the floor. "If you hadn't knocked on the door when you did, only God knows what would have happened. I'm so ashamed."

"Well, I'm glad I came up when I did. Don't beat yourself up too much Rose, you're not alone in this. I'll have a good talk with Vincent later."

"Oh, No! Please don't Ms. Weathersby! I'm not so innocent either. I think I love Vince."

"You think?" asked Ms. Weathersby.

"No, I'm sure I love him," said Rose.

"I'm trusting you Rose to do the right thing. Don't let a few moments of pleasure, turn into a lifetime of regret. Believe me, I may look like I don't know anything about sex, but I do. I've been down that road a few times before. I don't care how fine he is, or how smooth he talks, if he's not willing to buy the whole cow, then he can't have the milk, you remember that Rose."

"Yes, ma'am," Rose answered, feeling like a child. She thought; that sounds like something my grandma would say.

Before Ms. Weathersby left the room, she prayed with Rose then went downstairs.

Chapter 25

Bea was called to Warden Powell's office for the last time. She sat impatiently, waiting to know where her new home was going to be. Warden Powell shuffled some papers back and forth on his desk, then cleared his throat.

"Bea it seems your prayers are still being answered, there's an opening at The Farmington House for Women."

Bea was ecstatic. "Really you mean, I can live with Rose!"

"Well, I'm supposed to place you somewhere else, just call me a bleeding heart. I know Rose will be happy to have you with her again."

Bea jumped up and gave Warden Powell a huge hug.

"Thank You, Warden. I don't care what anyone says, you are the best."

"I've always cared for you Bea, for years I've watched your progress here. I've never declared myself to be a spiritual man, but I'm sure it's more than a coincidence that things turned out the way they did for you and Rose. I can truly say I'm happy to have known the two of you."

Bea smiled and then thanked him again.

"I always knew I had a guardian angel, Warden. I just never knew that he would be you."

He laughed. "Well I've never been called an angel before, but I do know right from wrong. I also believe in helping someone who tries to do the right things."

"Well Warden, if you keep it up your going to get a reputation for being a good man."

"Well I can't have that now can I, Bea," they both laughed.

"Bea asked, in a more serious manner. "Warden is there anything that can be done for Lee Anne and Big Bertha?"

Warden Powell scratched his head. "Well now Bea, Lee Anne doesn't have much time to go but, Bertha, on the other hand, it's going to take another one of those miracles to change her situation.

"Well, I'll keep praying for her anyhow, it worked for me."

"Now look Bea, in two days you'll be leaving here, I'll say my goodbye's now. He kissed her on the cheek and said goodbye.

Bea was shocked for a moment, then she spoke, "goodbye Warden Powell, God Bless You." She went back to her cell with a smile. Bea thought about just how good God really was.

Chapter 26

In spite of Rose asking Ms. Weathersby not to say anything to Vince, she did so anyway. She went downstairs to the kitchen and found Vince busy preparing dinner as usual.

"Mum, dinner isn't ready yet."

Ms. Weathersby spoke quickly. "Vincent I'd like to talk to you for a moment."

He continued working, "sure, what's up?"

"Have a seat."

"What about dinner?"

"This won't take long I'm concerned about you and Rose.

"Concerned?" asked Vince, sitting down slowly.

"Yes, I know it's not my business, and you and Rose are adults. But I need to know how you feel about her.

Vince looked puzzled.

"Mum, I've been with you a long time, and I've never known you to beat around the bush. What's wrong?"

"Vincent, I've never known anyone to catch your attention as much as Rose. Maybe you should slow down a bit.

Vince answered. "Slow it down? Mum, you know I've been looking for someone, like Rose, for a long time. And now that I've found her, I don't want to lose her."

"That may be so but, I don't want you two making a mistake you'll be paying for the rest of your life. There are some things worth waiting for, you know."

Vince looked surprised. "Why would you say that? Did Rose say I did something wrong?"

"Now what do you think, Vincent?"

Vince lowered his head, then spoke, "I simply let her know how I felt about her."

"Did you let her know in words or in action," asked Ms. Weathersby?

"It may have been both. I love her. I even told her so."

Vince got up from his seat, "here let me show you something."

He removed from the drawer, a small box, which held a beautiful diamond ring. He showed it to Ms. Weathersby.

"Vincent, it's beautiful, where did you get such a ring?"

"It was my mother's wedding ring; she took it off when my dad left us. It's all I have left to remember her by, and I'm going to give it to Rose when I ask her to marry me."

Vince took the ring and then placed it back in its box.

Teary-eyed, Ms. Weathersby grabbed a napkin then blew her nose.

"Vincent, that's wonderful! I've seen how you two have been acting around here. Don't think you fooled an old lady. If you're serious about marrying Rose, then you should ask her."

Vince grabbed Ms. Weathersby's hands.

"You don't think I blew it? I don't want her to think the wrong thing about me."

"Well, I don't know Vincent, she may not want to see you right now. All of those good looks, and charm, may have been a bit too much for her."

Vince leaned back against the chair.

"No, I really messed up, didn't I?"

"Oh, cheer up man, I'm only kidding with you. I don't know who's worst, you or Rose. And by the way, Rose love's you too."

Vince smiled.

"She told you that?"

"Yes, she did. Well, I'll let you get back to work, or dinner will be really late tonight."

Vince grabbed Ms. Weathersby from her chair then gave her a hug spinning her around.

"Put me down boy before I get dizzy," she said.

"She loves me! How wonderful? I must go see her."

"Hold it, Mister, you have work to do. You can see Rose at the dinner table.

Vince kissed her on the cheek. "Thanks for everything, Mum."

Rose stayed quiet at dinner. Vince tried getting her attention a few times, she wouldn't look at him. Ms. Weathersby noticed the cold shoulder Rose gave him and thought she would help him out.

"Rose, please help Vincent with the dishes after dinner?"

Vince mouthed the words thank you to Mrs. Weathersby, without anyone seeing.

Rose frowned then whispered to her, "I can't be alone with him."

Ms. Weathersby whispered back, "You'll be fine."

After dinner, Rose walked in the kitchen hesitantly, carrying a load of stacked plates from the dinner table. Vince walked over to help her, she quickly placed them on the table.

"Thank you, Vince, but, if you remember, I already owe Ms. Weathersby for broken dishes."

He laughed. Rose didn't. He noticed the sternness in her voice, it saddened him to see her acting the way she was. Rose started loading the dishwasher as quickly as possible.

Without wasting any more time, he went over to the drawer, took out the box, walked over to Rose, then placed the box in her hand. She stared at it. "What's this?"

"Open it, said Vince.

Rose opened the box and saw the ring. "Vince, it's beautiful."

He then knelt down on one knee, took her hand, then asked, "Rose, will you marry me?"

Rose put her hand over her mouth to keep from screaming, "OH MY GOD! Vince! Are you serious? Will I marry you!"

Rose hesitated, for a second.

YES!" she screamed.

She grabbed him around his neck, kissed him, and then ran out.

"I've got to show the others."

Rose pushed open the kitchen door. Suddenly Candy, Violet, and Stacey fell onto the dining room floor. Ms. Weathersby and Clara quickly sat down to the dining room table, pretending they weren't listening. Vince laughed at the three on the floor, then went back into the kitchen. Rose rushed over to Ms. Weathersby, showing her the ring on her finger.

"Ms. Weathersby!" she said excitedly, "look, isn't it beautiful, Vince asked me to marry him?"

Ms. Weathersby stood up slowly and gave her a hug. "That's wonderful, Rose. I told you it would be fine."

The girls rushed over to see the ring.

Violet asked, "Man! Rose, what did you do to get this?"

Ms. Weathersby butted in, "Violet! What a terrible thing to ask!"

"I didn't mean anything by it."

"Oh, she's just jealous," said Candy.

Violet yelled, "I said! I didn't mean anything by it!"

Rose smiled, then answered, "I guess I did something right."

Ms. Clara finally spoke. "Willie looks like there's going to be a wedding."

Everyone froze and looked at Ms. Weathersby. She laughed. "Yes, Clara, there's going to be a wedding."

Clara yawned. "How nice, I'm going to bed, all this excitement has made me tired."

Vince poked his head out the kitchen, "can I come out now?"

Rose went over to him, placed her arms around his shoulder, and kissed him again. Vince stood still with his eyes closed a few more seconds after the kiss was over. Rose touched his face, "goodnight Mr.

Vincent Hamlin. Rose turned to go upstairs. Vince turned to go with her but, Ms. Weathersby grabbed his arm.

"Whoa mister, you're not married yet."

Candy and the girls laughed, then went upstairs.

Ms. Weathersby asked, "Well, I guess we can all turn in right, Vincent?" Vince watched as Rose walked all the way up the stairs.

Ms. Weathersby spoke again. "I guess we can turn in now right, Vincent?"

Vince finally snapped out of his trance. "Uh yes, sure Mum."

Ms. Weathersby shook her head, thinking to herself, he's got it bad. "Have a good night Vince," she said.

Chapter 27

The next afternoon like clockwork, the mailman delivered the mail. As usual, Candy retrieved it before anyone else.

"Rose more mail for you!" yelled candy.

Rose hurried downstairs to see who it was from. She grabbed the mail from Candy's hand and began reading the envelopes. One letter was from the Boston Commissioners Office. The other was from Sis. Mona. She quickly opened the letter from Sis. Mona and began to read.

Rose screamed, "Ms. Weathersby! Vince! Everyone! I can't believe it!" Vince and Candy ran in to see what was wrong. Rose shouted, tears welling up in her eyes.

"They're letting my mom out of prison!"

Vince grabbed Rose, and spun her around, "that's wonderful Rose but, how is that possible? I thought she was in for life?"

Rose laughed with excitement. "I'll explain it the best I can."

Before she began, Ms. Clara and Ms. Weathersby came in. Rose yelled, "Ms. Weathersby, isn't it wonderful, my mom is getting out of prison soon!"

"Yes, Rose, I know."

"You know? How would you know? I just got a letter."

"I wanted it to be a surprise, Rose. The prison board contacted me a couple of days ago. Since Patrice is no longer living with us, they will allow your mother to stay here.

Rose yelled again, "staying here? She'll be staying here?" She began to cry and laugh at the same time. "Thank You God, for answering my prayer. I'm going to see my mother again. I haven't been this happy in a long time. I must be dreaming, somebody pinch me."

Candy pinched Rose's arm.

"Ow! Candy that was only a figure of speech."

Stacey pulled Rose over to the side then whispered, "Rose, how can I get to know your God? It seems He's always there for you. How can I get him to look out for me like that?"

Rose stared at Stacey for a moment. "Excuse me, everyone."

Clara spoke with disappointment. "Rose, I want to hear more about your mother?"

"We'll be right back."

Rose took Stacey in the living room then sat her down. She took her by the hands and began to pray.

"Alright Stacey, what I can tell you is this, I didn't want to hear about God. Praying or even going to church was not a part of my life. Thanks to my mom and Sis. Mona, I found out all about who God was and why I needed Him in my life. All I did was say that I believe Jesus is the Son of God and, that He died and rose again in order for me to be saved."

"Was it that simple, Rose?"

"Well, that was only the beginning Stacey, I also studied my bible. The more I studied, the more I wanted to know about the Father. The one thing I did find out was that God will meet you where you are. If He sees you trying, He will help you if you ask, and many times if you don't. Sunday when we go to church you can speak with, Pastor Clayton. He can explain it to you better than I.

"Okay, Rose I will, thanks.

Stacey gave Rose a hug then they went back into the dining room with the others.

"Vince, you can have her back now."

Vince grabbed Rose by the hand then took her out once again.

Candy protested, "Rose, you didn't tell us how your mom was getting out!"

Rose handed Candy the letter to read for herself. Stacey and Violet ran over to read the letter with Candy.

"Rose, this is unbelievable!" said Candy.

Ms. Clara argued. "Will someone please tell me how Rose's mother got out?"

"Come, Clara, I'll tell you all about it. Don't upset yourself," said Ms. Weathersby.

Candy turned to Rose. "Rose I'm so happy for you really I am. It must be a good feeling to know you're going to see your mother again."

Candy started to cry, "I never got the chance to know my mother at all."

Violet commented in disgust. "Alright, here it comes, once a year Candy has herself pity party for herself."

Rose gave Candy a hug. "I understand how you feel Candy, for years I didn't know my mother was even alive but, please don't cry, no one is allowed to be unhappy today okay."

She lifted Candy's head and smiled. "I'm going to need my maid of honor to be as pretty as possible for my wedding."

Candy perked up. "Maid of honor, you mean it, Rose?"

"Sure Candy. You're like a sister to Vince, it's appropriate that the groom's sister be in the wedding."

"Stacey asked, what about us?"

"Well, I will need bridesmaids. How about it, Violet? Do you think you could handle that?"

Violet looked at Rose with a stone face.

"What does a bridesmaid do?"

Rose answered, "Nothing, but look pretty."

"I can do that," Violet snapped her finger then switched upstairs.

Vince grabbed Rose's hand again and took her in the kitchen. He sat down with her at the table.

"Vince, what's wrong?"

With a look of concern on his face, Vince asked, "Rose, what if your mother doesn't like me, or doesn't want you to marry me? She doesn't know me, or my family, we've only been together a short time. What if?"

Rose placed her finger up to his lips, "shush, you have nothing to worry about. Bea is not like that. You do have one thing in your favor."

Vince posed like Mr. Olympic, flexing his muscles, "and what might that be? My charm, or my dashing good looks.

Rose laughed. "You can cook."

"Surely, you're kidding?"

He dropped his arms.

"No, I'm not my mother will tell you herself she has a weakness for a man who can cook."

"Well, I better start planning her welcome home dinner now. What's her favorite dish?"

"She doesn't have one. She likes all food. Whatever you cook, my mom will love it."

Rose had almost forgotten about the letter from the Boston Commissioner's Office. She couldn't imagine what it was about. She nervously tore it open.

"Ms. Weathersby!" She yelled.

Ms. Weathersby ran into the kitchen.

"Rose, what in the world is wrong with you, girl."

Rose spoke excitedly.

"The Boston Police Department is giving me some kind of award for helping them! Everyone is invited to come! Its next week. Isn't it great?! My mom will be home by then!"

Vince smiled. "Looks like all your dreams are coming true, Rose."

"Not dreams, Vince, blessings!" said Rose.

Ms. Clara started upstairs. "Well, all I know is, I can't handle any more good news today. I'm too old for this much excitement."

Chapter 28

"Captain, the Commissioner is on the line."

Morton picked up the phone. "Good Morning Commissioner sir."

"Good Morning Captain Dunn. We can cut the formalities."

"Yes, Sir," said Morton.

"The reward for the capture of Culpepper is pretty substantial. Are you sure you want to give it all to this Rose Hill girl?"

"Yes, Commissioner absolutely, she's earned every dime of it. We couldn't have caught him that quick without her."

"Well, the check is here from the First National Loan and Finance Company. I'm looking at $50.000. I'll present it to her during the ceremony."

Morton asked, "Commissioner, will you allow me to present the reward to Ms. Hill instead?"

"Well, I don't see a problem with it, but there are others we wanted to give awards too."

"I'm familiar with Ms. Hills background Commissioner. I know she's had a tough life and, I just wanted to be the first one to congratulate her and say good luck." Morton thought to himself, and to say I'm sorry is more like it. Morton's thoughts were interrupted when the commissioner spoke. "Well, I don't see any harm it would do. You can make the presentation to Ms. Hill last, so it won't throw off the ceremony with us changing places."

"Thanks, Commissioner. I'm sure Ms. Hill will be happy."

Morton hung up the phone and leaned back in his chair, thinking of Rose once again. I haven't seen Rose in almost 4 years now. I wonder if she's changed much. I couldn't bring myself to see her after the Culpepper bust. I really hope receiving this money would ease some of the pain I've caused her. I'll never forget the look she gave me when they took her away that night. If only I could get her to forgive me. She didn't deserve what happened to her.

Officer Jones barged into the office interrupting Morton's thoughts.

"Sorry Captain but, I kept telling this lady you were busy. She says she's your neighbor. One thing she is; is hard of hearing."

Morton let out a sigh as he sat up in his chair.

"It's okay Jones; I'll take it from here."

Ms. Jackson sat in one of the chairs and crossed her legs. She grabbed a file from Morton's desk and began to fan with it. "Hot isn't it?"

Morton grabbed the file from her hand in anger. "Ms. Jackson, why are you here?"

Ms. Jackson looked at Morton then started to cry. "I know I shouldn't have come here, but I couldn't think of anything else to do. Why don't you like me? I've done all I can to make you like me. I know you're not married or committed to anyone. Don't you find me attractive?"

Ms. Jackson reached inside her handbag for a tissue. I need to know now, are we ever going to get together?"

Morton sat back in his chair. "Ms. Jackson," he said calmly. "I am very sorry if I've offended you in any way. I think you are a very attractive woman."

"You do?" she said surprised.

"Yes, I do." Morton raised from his seat, walked around his desk, and sat on the edge of it. He lifted her up from her seat, and while escorting her to the door, he continued talking to her calmly and slowly.

"You know, I don't even know your first name."

"It's Marla," she said with a girlish grin."

"I'll tell you what Marla. I'm going to have one of the officer's escort you home. I want you to pick out one of your finest dresses. I'm going to take you out to dinner tonight. Would you like that, Marla?"

"Yes, I would." Ms. Jackson grabbed Morton's hands. "You're not just toying with me are you Officer Dunn?"

"I most certainly am not. You have my word as a gentleman." Morton raised Ms. Jackson's hands and kissed them softly.

Ms. Jackson giggled again.

"Okay tonight at 7:00 P.M. Don't be late, she added happily."

"I won't," Morton answered.

Morton opened the door and beckoned for one of the officers to take her home. Officer Jones snarled as she walked by. Ms. Jackson walked past his desk smiling without noticing him.

Officer Jones asked, "Captain who was that loon?"

Morton responded, "Jones haven't you got any manners? That lady could very well be the future Mrs. Morton Dunn."

Morton walked back inside his office and let out a laugh. Officer Jones sat in silence and shook his head.

Chapter 29

Finally, the day had come for Bea to be released. She said goodbye to all the ladies whether she knew them or not. Sis. Mona held a special going away bible class in her honor. Each lady stood and told of the first time they encountered Bea. Big Bertha spoke last.

"Well, most of you know I'm not much for words." Big Bertha spoke softly looking down at the floor. One of the ladies shouted from the back.

"We can't hear you, Bert, back here! Speak up!"

Bertha raised her head in anger. "If you take the wax out your ears Pearl, then you can hear!"

Big Bertha frowned then looked over at Bea. Bea smiled and nodded for Bertha to continue. Big Bertha cleared her throat and started to speak again.

"Over the years, people have come and gone from this place. It never bothered me, 'cause, I knew my best friend was still here with me. Well, that's not going to be true anymore."

Bea stopped smiling. She took a piece of tissue from her pocket and wiped her eyes.

"I never cared much for people. I guess with my husband cheating on me and my family deserting me, I never expected I'd be able to trust anybody again. Well, I was wrong. Over twenty years ago Bea came to this place. We hit it off right away. I liked her because she had balls and, besides Rose, she was the only one to stand up to me."

Sis. Mona cleared her throat.

"Sorry, Sis. Mona. I meant she had courage. Bea told me when I was wrong, which was many times." Everyone laughed. "But, most of all she was always straight with me. I've never had to watch my back around her. I'm going to miss her more than my own sister."

With tears welling up in her eyes. Big Bertha pulled out of her bosom the communion wine.

"Here's to you, Bea."

Big Bertha turned up the bottle to take a drink. Sis Mona rushed over and grabbed it from her hands.

"Bertha! What are you doing with that? Shame on you! Taking the Lord's wine for your own enjoyment."

"I was just making a toast to my girl Sis. Mona. I was gonna put it back." exclaimed Bertha with her fingers crossed behind her back.

"Well, you won't have to worry about putting it back now, I'll do it for you. And by the way Bertha, you wouldn't happen to know what happened to the other wine that came up missing a little while ago when Rose left?"

Big Bertha grinned, "Well no, can't say that I do."

"I hope you're right, Bertha," said Sis. Mona.

Bea walked up to Bertha and gave her a big hug.

"Bert that was a wonderful speech I didn't know you had it in you."

Bertha whispered, "Bea, do you think she knows it was me who took the wine the first time?"

"I wouldn't worry about it, Bert. If she was going to do something. It would have already been done."

"Yeah, you're right," said Big Bertha relieved.

"Bert, I never knew you felt like that about me. I mean, me being like your sister and all. It really touched my heart to hear you say that. I feel you're like a sister to me too."

Bea hugged Big Bertha again.

"I'm really going to miss you, Bert. I'll be praying for you. Just keep your nose clean. And don't take any more communion wine."

"You know Bea I'll be praying for you too as best I can."

Bea and Bertha both left the classroom teary-eyed. They walked to Bertha's cell first.

"So long Bea," Bertha said with a half-smile.

"So long my sister," said Bea as she walked to her cell.

Bert sat, on her bunk and turned her back to the bars of her cell. She wiped her eyes. Lee Anne walked in.

"Bert are you okay?" she asked.

Startled, Bertha jumped around staring at Lee Anne. "No, I'm not," said Bertha sadly.

Lee Anne didn't know what to do. She never saw Big Bertha act that way. She sat beside her on her bunk in silence. Bea quickly gathered up her things. The things she couldn't carry, she left to Big Bertha and Lee Ann. Thelma was pleased to be the guard to escort Bea out.

"This is it, Thelma, said Bea happily. So, you're doing me the honors eh."

"Yes Bea, this is it."

Bea looked around her cell for the last time.

"Tell me something Thelma, how come I feel like I'm going to miss this place?"

"The way I see it, Bea, this has been your home for over twenty years. I'm sure it's more the people you're gonna miss, rather than the place. I figure it's only natural what you feel."

"I guess you're right Thelma."

"You know Bea, you never gave me a problem in here. Matter of fact, you made my job a little easier. I know the other guards feel the same way. They respected you and your opinion. I'd like to personally thank you from all of us."

Thelma pulled out an envelope.

"This is from the guards. It's not much, but it will help you get a couple of outfits when you get out. The styles have changed a bit since you came in."

"Oh, thank you, Thelma, this is wonderful. Tell the others I said thanks, okay."

"Sure Bea," said Thelma.

Bea placed the envelope in her bosom and pushed passed Thelma. "Now let me out of here, before they change their minds."

Sis. Mona waited at the gate to say her final goodbyes to Bea.

"Give Rose a big hug from me when you see her. And tell her to keep praying. The best is yet to come."

The bus pulled up right on schedule. Bea looked around one last time.

"Open the gate!" Yelled the guard.

"Thank You Sister, if it hadn't been for you and your guidance, I don't think I'd be here today."

"Well one thing I do know Bea is, what God has for you is for you. No one can take that away from you."

"Keep an eye on Bertha for me. She'll need you. She's not as big and bad as she pretends to be."

"I know, and don't worry about Bertha she'll be just fine. As long as she stays away from my communion wine." They both laughed. Bea walked out and stepped on the bus. She waved to Sis. Mona from her window then sat back.

"I'm on my way Rose I can't wait to see you again."

Chapter 30

Rose fumbled around her room, anxiously.

"What time is it?" She peeked into the hall. Can somebody tell me what the time is?"

"Rose, don't you have a clock in your room?" Stacey asked as she walked by. If I can remember right, there is a clock in there." Stacey peeked inside Roses room. There it is Rose right over the desk."

"Thanks, Stacey, I didn't see it. I must have knocked it over."

Rose checked her hair once again. Stacey noticed how nervous she was. "Rose, why are you so nervous?"

"You know Stacey, I never thought this day would come. That, my Mom and I would ever see each other again. Let alone live in the same home. I just can't believe this is happening. I just want everything to be perfect for her first day out."

"I'm sure it will be Rose. Just take it easy."

"I'd better check on dinner just in case Vince needs my help."

Rose darted out her room. Stacey watched Rose as she ran down the stairs.

"Vince needing help with the cooking, that's a new one." Stacey laughed to herself then went downstairs. Rose raced into the kitchen.

"How's everything going, Vince?" Rose asked, trying not to appear worried."

"Just great Rose, I'm almost done with everything. Except, I can't seem to get my gravy right for my smothered chicken. And the watermelon is a bit sour for my fruit salad. And I."

Rose screamed. "No! Nothing can go wrong today, Vince! Everything has got to be perfect!"

Vince grabbed Rose by her shoulders. "Rose, I was just kidding. Calm down. I have everything under control." He walked her to the kitchen door. Now, go fix your hair before your mom gets here."

Rose was on the other side of the kitchen door before she realized what he said. She yelled. "Fix my hair! What's wrong with my hair?"

Vince yelled back. "I was just kidding!"

Rose turned to the door with her hands on her hips. "This is no time to be kidding Vince!

Ms. Weathersby came into the dining room. "What is all the yelling about?"

"Vince seems to feel this is a time to joke around. When my mother will be here at any moment now. He knows I want everything to be perfect."

"Come here, Rose. You're going to have to calm down or you'll have an anxiety attack. Vince knows what he's doing. Now the bus should be arriving any moment now. And I would rather you let Candy and Stacey meet your mother at the bus."

Rose protested. "Why can't I meet her! I've waited too long already!"

"Let Candy and Stacey meet her Rose. I wouldn't want you to get hit by a car before you get to her."

"I don't think I can wait any longer," Rose said, wringing her hands.

"Well, come and give me a hand with my zipper. My arthritis won't let me reach too far behind me."

Rose followed her into her room. She looked around. "I've never been in here before."

Ms. Weathersby stood in front of the mirror and put on her earrings. Rose zipped her dress. She walked around Ms. Weathersby's room, looking at the old pictures.

"Who is this?" Rose asked, holding the picture frame.

"That's me and my older sister."

"You have a sister?"

"I had a sister. That was a long time ago. Now let's check on dinner."

Ms. Weathersby left her room with Rose still inside. Rose stared at the picture a little longer. She knew there was no point in prying. If Ms. Weathersby wanted to tell her more about her family, she would in her own time. Why do I feel like I've seen this before? Rose dismissed her thoughts, placed the picture back on the dresser, and left the room.

Chapter 31

The bus ride was a bumpy one. Bea's heart pumped fast. She was too excited to sleep although she was tired. Everything has changed so much in 20 years, she thought. There aren't many buildings I recognize that's still standing before I went in. The High school I went to is still there, Ansbury High. Man does that bring back a lot of old memories. The library, the old Boston Bank Building. Lord, look at the way the women dress now. If you dressed like that in my day, you were considered to be one thing, and that was it. They surely don't leave anything to the imagination.

Bea heard music playing. The bus driver answered his phone. So that's what those little phones look like. The cars are much nicer looking. I wonder if I can still drive. I have so much to learn now that I'm out. The technology today is much more advanced and I don't know how to use any of it. I sure am hungry. I should have eaten when I had the chance back in joint. I hope this Vince cooks as good as Rose claims. Although anything is better than prison food. Bea yelled to the Bus driver.

"Driver! How much longer before we reach downtown Boston?"

"Not long Miss," he answered.

Bea pulled out her small pocket bible given to her by Sis. Mona.

"Well, I'll read a bit to pass the time."

Bea looked out the window once more and smiled. "Jessie, if you can hear me, I'm free. And, I'm going to be with Rose once again."

Vince sat the last dish on the dining table. "Alright now the table is set. All that's missing is our guest of honor."

"Vincent, you've outdone yourself. The table is beautiful," said Ms. Weathersby.

"I've spared no expense for my future Mother-In-Law. Oh my, that's the first time I've said that. I'm actually going to meet Rose's mother for the first time." Vince grabbed his head.

"Vince are you alright?" asked Ms. Weathersby, helping him to a chair.

"Mum, I really never thought I'd meet Rose's mother. What if she doesn't like me?"

Rose entered the dining room, answering Vince's question.

"Of course, she'll have to taste your cooking before she decides if you're good enough for me or not," Rose smirked.

"Rose, that is not funny," said Vince.

"Weren't you full of jokes a moment ago, Mr. Funny Man?"

Vince stood from his chair. "Funny Man? Who are you calling names?"

"You see Ms. Weathersby he wants to start an argument!"

Vince yelled, "an argument! Whose arguing?"

Rose walked over closer to where Vince was standing. She placed her hands on her hips. Before she could say anything, the doorbell rang.

"Saved by the bell," mumbled Ms. Weathersby. "Rose, Vincent, you two stop it now! You both sound foolish. You're just nervous, that's all."

"She's right, Vince. I am nervous. I'm sorry. I don't want to argue."

"I'm sorry too Rose. I'm a bit nervous myself. Forgive me?"

Rose placed her hand on Vince's cheek. "I can't stay angry with you. My mother is going to love you. Don't worry."

Vince hugged and kissed Rose. Ms. Weathersby walked to the door and opened it.

"Never mind, I'll get the door, she said, shaking her head.

Ms. Weathersby opened the door slowly. Bea stood about to ring the bell again.

Well, I'll be! "You must be Rose's mother, Bea. Come in! I'm Ms. Weathersby head of Farmington House."

Ms. Weathersby looked past Bea looking down the street.

"I sent a welcoming party to meet you. I wonder where the girls are?"

Bea stepped in, looking around. "Is this where Rose Hill lives?"

"Yes, Bea," said Ms. Weathersby, you have the right place. Before she could call for Rose to come, Rose ran to the door.

"Bea!" She screamed. "You're finally here!"

"Rose! How wonderful. You're just like I remembered, beautiful."

Bea and Rose hugged, laughing and crying at the same time.

"Ladies, I'm sorry to interrupt but, did you see two young ladies standing around the bus station with a sign?

"There were quite a few young ladies just standing around."

"Well, I guess there would be. The bus station is usually where you can find runaways or homeless girls."

"But, these two girls would have been carrying a sign with your name on it."

"Come to think about it, I did see two girls carrying a sign on my way here. I didn't notice if it had my name on it or not."

"I sent them to meet you."

Bea apologized, "I'm sorry when the bus pulled in, I grabbed the first cab I saw. I couldn't wait to see my Rose."

Ms. Weathersby stepped out on the porch to look down the street again.

"Never mind, here they come!"

Candy came running up on the porch first. Out of breath, she shouted, "Mum, she wasn't there!"

Stacey came up running behind her. "She's right, Ms. Weathersby! We asked around! She was not there!"

"It's alright girls she's here."

Puzzled Candy asked, "She's here? What do you mean she's here? You mean we went for nothing?"

Bea spoke softly. I'm sorry ladies. I took a cab here. I didn't know Ms. Weathersby sent out a welcoming party for me. I thank you both."

Stacey spoke first. "It's okay Ms. Bea anything for Rose's mother."

"Yeah, we needed the exercise. Some more than others," added Candy looking at Stacey from behind."

"Speak for yourself," grunted Stacey.

"Uh hum," Vince cleared his throat.

Rose grabbed Vince by the arm and then escorted him to Bea.

"Bea, uh Mom, this is Vince, the man I was talking about in my letter. Whom I love very much and who asked me to marry him."

Bea circled around Vince sizing him up. Ms. Weathersby stood by and watched.

"Marry, Huh? Rose, you didn't mention anything about getting married. Nor, did you mention how fine this young man was. I've been locked up a long time but, I know a good-looking man when I see one."

Bea grabbed Vince and gave him a hug.

"You must be very special for Rose to fall in love with."

"Thank you for saying that, Ms. Bea. I know I haven't known Rose very long but, falling in love with her was the best thing that could have happened to me. Now that I have met you, it would please me if you would give us your blessing to be married."

Bea looked over at Rose. "Rose, you didn't tell me he had an accent. Where you from son?"

"I'm from London, England, mum."

"England huh, aren't you a long way from home?"

"No Mum, this is my home."

Candy snickered at how nervous Vince appeared. Rose intervened.

"That's enough interrogation for now Ma. Vince made a wonderful dinner for you."

"Yes, that's right Bea," said Ms. Weathersby. "I'll show you where to put your things, then we'll all sit and have dinner."

"That's fine with me, I'm starved," said Bea, following Ms. Weathersby.

Rose and Vince walked in the kitchen.

"You see Vince she's not so bad, is she?"

Vince lowered his head. "I don't think she likes me."

"Now, why would you say that?"

"She doesn't like the way I talk."

Rose spoke softly trying to sound reassuring.

"Bea's never heard a British accent before Vince. She didn't mean anything by it. Don't worry. Besides, I love the way you talk."

Candy bolted in the kitchen door. "Everyone is seated at the table. Can we eat now?"

"We're coming," answered Rose. "Come on now Vince cheer up."

"I'll be alright."

Rose tried kissing Vince's cheek, he turned and kissed her on the lips.

"Well, I see someone is feeling fine."

"Kiss me again and I'll be fine and dandy."

"Get a room!" Candy uttered, then left the kitchen.

"I think we'd better go now, Vince."

"It's not fair to start something you can't finish, Rose" whispered Vince.

"I was merely trying to cheer you up," said Rose softly.

"You've succeeded. Now I'm going to have to wait a moment to become less cheery."

Rose laughed then joined the others.

Chapter 32

Bea pushed herself back from the dining table and patted her stomach.

"Vincent, the dinner was excellent. And it was not because I was hungry either. I haven't enjoyed food like that since my late husband," Bea stopped speaking in mid-sentence. "Well, for a very long time," she said with reservation. "I do thank you for going through all this trouble. You'll have to give me that clam chowder recipe. It was to die for."

Bea stopped speaking again and looked at Rose. Rose smiled.

"It's okay Bea, said Ms. Weathersby everyone here knows why you were in prison. We're not here to judge."

Clara waved from the other end of the table. "Bea dear, Willie told me you are Rose's mother. It's so nice to have you here especially, since the nursing home bust and all."

Bea looked puzzled. "Rose, what does she mean nursing home bust? And who is Willie?

Rose whispered. "Willie is Ms. Weathersby. She doesn't like to be called that. I didn't tell you about my involvement with the police because I didn't want to worry you.

"Police! Rose what happened!"

"It's okay now. I was helping the police for a while when I was working at the nursing home down the street. I did such a good job they want to give me an award or something next week."

Bea looked worried. "Are you sure everything is okay Rose?"

"Yes, I'm sure Ma, there's nothing to worry about, it's over."

"You should have been here, Ms. Bea," said Candy excitedly. "It was in the papers and everything!"

"Candy, that's enough talk, said Ms. Weathersby. "You, Violet and Stacey clear the table and do the dishes."

"Do the dishes? But it's Rose's turn! Candy stomped.

Ms. Weathersby cut Candy a dirty look. Violet and Stacey stood to clear the table.

"There's nothing to worry about Bea. Rose made us all proud. The Boston Police Department is giving Rose an award for helping them, and they invited us all to come and be a part of the awards ceremony. You couldn't have come at a better time."

"Well, I never would have thought Rose would help the police. If you say, there's nothing to worry about I won't."

"Come, Bea, let me show you to your room. You can take Patrice's old room."

"Who is Patrice?" Bea asked.

Rose and Ms. Weathersby looked at each other.

Rose answered, "Patrice used to live here, Bea. I'll tell you about her some other time."

Ms. Weathersby noticed Clara had gone to sleep at the table again.

"Lord, that woman can't put a crumb of food in her mouth without going to sleep after she eats it. Rose show Bea to her room and, I'll put Clara to bed."

Bea laughed when she saw Ms. Weathersby struggle to get Clara awake.

"Come on, Clara, time for bed."

"Already? I'm not tired."

"Well, if you're not tired then, you can help with the dishes."

Miss Clara yawned. "Well, I guess I am a wee bit tired. A couple minutes of a nap might do me some good."

"Goodnight Miss Clara," said Bea smiling.

Bea turned to Rose. "Rose, I think I'm going to like it here."

Bea picked up her belongings then, slowly walked towards the hall looking around. She noticed the sign. You dirty it! You clean it! She laughed. "Somebody has a good sense of humor."

"Believe me, Bea, Ms. Weathersby is very serious about that. And please don't break anything. I already owe forty dollars for broken dishes."

"Forty dollars for dishes?"

"Don't ask Ma it's a long story."

Bea laughed again. She peeped into Ms. Weathersby room. "Whose room is this? It's nice."

Before Rose could answer, Bea walked inside.

Rose grabbed Bea by her arm. "Ma, this is Ms. Weathersby's room come out of here before she catches you."

Bea walked over to the chest of drawers and picked up the picture frame with Ms. Weathersby and her sister. "What's she doing with my mother's picture?"

What do you mean your mother's picture? Come on, Ma let's go."

Rose started pulling Bea toward the door.

"No, Rose I'm serious. This is your Grandma Jessie and her sister."

Ms. Weathersby walked into her room. "Rose? Bea? Why are you in my room?"

Bea turned to Ms. Weathersby, holding up the picture frame. "Where did you get my mother's picture?"

"Your mother's picture?" Ms. Weathersby walked over and then snatched the picture frame from Bea's hand. "I've had this picture since I was a little girl."

Bea grabbed her bag and poured all her belongings out onto the bed.

"Ma what are you doing?"

"I know, I have it here someplace. Bea rummaged through all the photographs of Jessie and Rose. I know I'm not imagining things."

Slowly Bea pulled out the snapshot of Jessie and her sister. She showed it to Ms. Weathersby first.

"It's the exact same picture Bea, where did you get this? There were only two. I had one, and my sister had one."

Bea asked, "Ms. Weathersby, by any chance was your big sister named Jessie?"

"Yes, it was. How did you know that? I've never told anyone about my sister. Where did you get this picture?"

Bea and Ms. Weathersby both stared at each other. Rose grabbed the two pictures and put them side by side.

Rose screamed. "They are the same! Don't you get it, Ma, Ms. Weathersby!" Rose pointed to the pictures. "You and my Grandma Jessie were sisters! That makes us your nieces! No wonder you favored my grandma! I thought that the first day I saw you. I was afraid to say something!

Rose looked at Bea and Ms. Weathersby grinning. They both sat speechless on the bed.

"Snap out of it you two, we're family!" Rose grabbed Bea and Ms. Weathersby and kissed them both on the cheek.

Bea continued to stare at Ms. Weathersby. "I never dreamed I had any other family, except Rose and Jessie. Jessie never mentioned you outside of this one picture."

Ms. Weathersby wiped a tear from her eye. "Jessie's daughter. I haven't said Jessie's name in almost forty years. When we were children, when they separated us, I promised Jessie I would find her, and we would be together again. I didn't know the first place to start looking. I couldn't find her. I didn't know the name of the family that had adopted her. I just assumed the family she was with moved out of state since I never saw her again. I guess she couldn't find me either. And, now as I live and breathe, I'm looking at her children, Bea and Rose. I couldn't be happier.

Ms. Weathersby grabbed both Bea and Rose and sobbed.

"I'm so sorry, Jessie," she cried. "I didn't look harder. Please forgive me Bea, Rose."

"Please don't cry Auntie, said Bea lifting her face and wiping her tears. This is a joyous occasion. I don't know anyone who is more blessed than we three are right now. You have nothing to be forgiven for. This was all divine timing."

Rose jumped off the bed. "I've got to tell Vince! He will not believe this! I can hardly believe it myself!"

Rose bolted out of Ms. Weathersby's room. The doorbell rang. Candy ran out of her room at the same time.

"I'll get it! yelled Candy."

Rose and Candy almost collided into each other. "Candy! Rose yelled. I'm your cousin!"

"Cousin? What are you talking about Rose?"

"Bea and I just found out that Ms. Weathersby is our Auntie! She was my Grandma's sister. How about that?!" Rose laughed.

The doorbell rang again. Vince stepped out of his room.

"Is someone getting the door?"

"Vince!" Rose yelled. "I have great news! Bea and I just found out that Ms. Weathersby is our Aunt!"

"What! How!"

"She and my Grandma Jessie were sisters! Bea and Ms. Weathersby had the same picture from when they were kids."

"You mean that photo on her bureau? The one she never talks about?"

"Yes, isn't it wonderful?" I have a real family now! Rose cried. "I have a real family! Thank You, God!"

Vince held her close and stroked her hair.

"God loves you, Rose, and so do I. I am so very happy for you."

The doorbell rang once again.

Bea and Ms. Weathersby came out of her room. Violet and Stacey came running down the stairs.

Violet asked, "why won't someone get the door?"

Candy ran over to Mrs. Weathersby. "Mum, is it true, what Rose said?"

"Is what true?" asked Stacey.

Candy was exasperated. She sighed.

"That Mum is Rose and Ms. Bea's aunt.

"What?! Both Violet and Stacey looked at each other.

"Yes, ladies, it's true." Ms. Weathersby explained, "I found out today that Bea's mother was my sister. That makes Bea my niece and Rose my great niece."

Chapter 33

Violet walked over to the door. "Well I better get the door, maybe that's somebody saying I hit the lottery." She spoke under her breath with sarcasm. "Since we're so blessed in this house." "Give me a break." She flung the door open. "Who is it?"

A distinguished looking man stood at the door. He removed his hat. "Good day, Mum. I'm seeking the whereabouts of Mr. Vincent Hamlin. Is this where he resides?"

Violet turned and yelled down the hall. "Vince there's someone at the door for you!" Vince excused himself from the others. "Yes, may I help you?"

At the door stood an elderly man wearing a traditional English derby holding a cane. He removed his derby before he spoke.

"How do you do, Sir? My name is Archibald Hancock. Are you Mr. Vincent Hamlin, son of Walter and Hannah Hamlin?"

"Yes, I am. What is this about?"

Mr. Hancock handed Vince an envelope.

"This sir is the last will and testament of Mr. Walter Hamlin. I am a private detective hired by your father's estate attorney to find you and your mother. I am very sorry it took so long to locate you. Your father was not aware that your mother was deceased. He wrote you and your mother a letter. I was instructed to give this to you or her depending upon who I found first."

Vince took the two-page letter and slowly opened it. All kinds of emotions ran through his mind. Anger, sadness, happiness, curiosity, got the better of him, so he opened the letter.

My Dearest Hannah,

Please forgive me. If you are reading this letter, then I must be dead; because only death could keep me from telling you this in person. Please know that I never meant to leave you and Vincent in that station. That was not my intent. I couldn't tell you that I allowed a perfect stranger to take our money; that took us so many years to save, and losing it on a silly card game. It looked so easy. I just knew I could win and double our money. He was in the men's room. I sent Vincent out to be with you. I didn't want you waiting for me alone. I only bet once, or twice and each time I won. I kept playing and won even more money but, the cards turned, and I started losing. At first, I told myself I could win it all back, and there would have been no harm done. However, the guy wouldn't let me continue to play with no money. So, I gave him my watch and then my wedding band. I couldn't believe I had lost everything in ten minutes. Our plan to open our own restaurant in America was gone. I couldn't face you or Vincent.

I had to do something before you became worried and started looking for me. I followed the man out of the train station. I tried to force him to give me my back money. He wasn't alone. They jumped me and knocked me out. I don't know how long I was out but, when I woke up, I was in a hospital. I couldn't remember anything. My papers were gone. I had no proof of identification. It took me weeks to regain my memory and realize I had a wife and son whom I had abandoned. I can only imagine what you and Vincent went through. I'm so very sorry. Please tell Vincent not to hate me for not being there. I went back to the station looking for you both. I knew you wouldn't be there, but I had to see for myself. I searched for days. I had no money. The authorities were of no help, they thought I made up the whole story. My only guess was that you and Vincent went back to England. I took odd jobs around the station until I had enough money for a train ticket to return home. I started a search for you at home to no avail. I almost lost my mind with worry. I couldn't sleep or eat. I almost died, and I would have if it had not been for Duncan. I saw him many times coming and going through the train station. We became friends. He knew of my peril. He offered me a job driving for his furniture company. I went from driving trucks to making furniture. It turned out I was really good at it. Duncan would say I was a natural. After months of successful sales from the furniture pieces I made, Duncan offered me a percentage of his business. It wasn't much at first, but, as time went on, I ventured out and started my own furniture company. You always said I was good with my hands, Hannah. I just never thought I would be so successful at it. I promised myself I would not frivolously spend any of the money I made. With the exception of food and shelter, I saved almost every dime I made. It's yours and Vincent's. I can't pay you for what I did. Please know I never stopped loving you and Vincent and I never stopped looking.

"What is this? This can't be true."

Vince slowly backed away from the door. Ms. Weathersby noticing the gentleman at the door, she walked up to see who he was.

Vince dropped the letter after reading its content. Ms. Weathersby picked it up and began to read it herself.

"Vincent, I'm so sorry. I don't think he knew your mother died some time ago. Vince that means you're the sole heir of his whole estate.

Vince turned to leave.

"I don't want his money!"

When Rose came up to the door, she took his hand. He stopped walking and fell to his knees. Holding his head in his hands, he began to cry.

"All these years I prayed for him to come and get us. All of the years, my mother cried because she thought he deserted us. Why couldn't he find us while she was alive, while he was alive?"

Rose looked at Bea. Bea smiled a sad smile. Ms. Weathersby kneeled down to console Vince. He didn't acknowledge her. Rose touched his cheeks and raised his head. She slowly wiped the tears from his eyes.

"You're not alone. We're your family now. Look around you." Rose pointed to Bea and Ms. Weathersby. "You have not one but two mothers." She looked over to Candy, Violet, and Stacey. "You have three sisters. And most of all you have me."

Vince smiled and hugged Rose. He held his arms out for the others to come over and give him a hug also. "You're so right, Rose, I have a wonderful family."

Vince stood then went back to the front door. "Please excuse, me sir for being rude. Would you like to come in?"

Mr. Hancock placed his hat back on his head.

"Thank You for your hospitality but, I must report back to your father's Estate Attorney to inform him that I found you. We will be in touch with you to go over the formalities of the Estate and how to receive your money. Mr. Hamlin put away quite a fortune. Six million dollars is a lot of money."

Vince shut the door behind Mr. Hancock and leaned against it. "Six million dollars?! Thank You, Dad!"

Chapter 34

Morton balled up several pieces of paper, throwing them in the trash. Some went inside, most did not. His mind raced with anticipation, trying to think of what he could say about Rose. Thoughts of seeing Rose again made him feel nervous. I wonder if she'll recognize me right away. I can't hardly wait to see her. The ringing doorbell broke his thoughts. He frowned and noticed the time. Walking to the door, he mumbled, "9 P.M., who could this be?"

He looked through the peephole and saw it was his neighbor, Marla.

"Marla? What do I owe this pleasure?"

Marla blushed. "Hello Morton, I hope I'm not disturbing you. I just wanted to thank you again for such a wonderful dinner the other night. I really had a good time. I brought over a bottle of wine for a nightcap. I hope you don't mind."

"No not at all, please come in."

Marla stepped in and looked around. This is nice and cozy Morty, I hope you don't mind me calling you that. Marla sat on the sofa and crossed and uncrossed her legs. Morton noticed how fidgety she was.

"Marla is there something wrong?"

Morton poured the wine and handed her a glass.

"Morty, I have a confession to make. I came over because I was hoping you would be home. I just didn't want to be alone tonight. I couldn't stop thinking about our date. I hope I don't sound silly. I just wanted to see you again."

Morton looked surprised. He lifted her from the sofa. "Oh, you wanted to see me, huh?"

Marla couldn't look him straight in his eyes. "I did but, you always seem so in a hurry, every time I see you."

Morton took the glass from her hand. "I'm not in a hurry now."

Morton moved Marla's hair off her neck then kissed it. She giggled and hit his chest. "Stop it you devil, I'm not that easy." He kissed her neck again. She backed away. Morton picked her up and laid her on the couch. She unbuttoned his shirt.

"Take me," she said.

In an instant, Morton's thoughts raced back to a conversation he had with Jessie. "I'd rather die than to let you take my Rose from me." He sat up on the side of the couch.

"Morty, what's wrong? Did I do something? Marla placed her hands around his head, trying to get his attention again.

"No, I'm sorry Marla, I just remembered something I have to do."

"Something you have to do. What? I don't understand."

Morton lifted Marla from the sofa. He helped her to the door. "Forgive me Marla, but I'm going to have to ask you to visit some other time. I know you don't understand, but there is something I have to do."

Marla fought back her tears. "I'm sorry if I disturbed you. It won't happen again." She then opened the door for herself and left.

Morton sat down at his desk, picked up his pen, and started to write once again. This time the words flowed.

Chapter 35

Farmington House was full of life. Everyone was hustling to get dressed for the awards ceremony. A feeling of joy flowed throughout the house. Everyone was downstairs except for Rose and Bea.

"Vince, please bring the van around." Ms. Weathersby yelled upstairs. "Alright everyone, we don't want to be late!"

Rose and Bea fussed around upstairs. Rose complained, "I don't like what I'm wearing. I can't wait to buy me some new clothes."

"Rose, you look just fine. You're one of a few women in this world who can wear anything and look good. Now I, on the other hand, am not."

Rose laughed, "You look good too, Ma."

Ms. Weathersby yelled upstairs again. "Bea! Rose! Let's go!"

Rose yelled back. "Coming!"

Bea laughed. "We'd better get downstairs before our Auntie bust a stitch."

Everyone piled in the van. Rose sat up front.

"Mum, say goodbye to this old van because I'm going to buy you a new SUV fully loaded."

"That's nice, Vincent but, you should plan for your wedding first."

"Don't worry about the money, Mum. My dad left me six million dollars!"

Everyone yelled at the same time. "Six million dollars!"

Rose looked at him with her mouth open. "Vince, why didn't tell me that your dad left you so much money?"

"I wanted to surprise you, Rose. Now you can go to medical school full time without a worry. It won't be easy, but nothing worth having ever is." Vince drove off humming to himself.

Ms. Clara asked, "Willie did I hear that boy, right? Did he say his dad left him six million dollars?"

This time Ms. Weathersby didn't cringe. "Yes, Clara, you heard him right."

"Well, where did he get it? Was he a crook or something? Where has he been all this time?"

Ms. Weathersby protested. "Clara, you ought to be ashamed of yourself asking such things."

Vince laughed. "It's okay Mum. It's hard for me to believe too. My dad tried to make up for leaving us. He'll never know that all we ever wanted was for him to come back. But, since that will never happen now, I'll use the money he left me to take care of my new family."

Candy, Violet, and Stacey sang. "We are family! I got all my sisters with me!" Bea and Rose joined in.

Once arriving at the Civic Center, Rose grew nervous. "There are so many police cars here."

They entered the center and found the room where the ceremony was being held. The seats for the recipients and their families were roped off.

Clara and the girls sat together. Rose sat with Bea, Vince, and Ms. Weathersby.

Bea whispered, "Rose, this is so exciting to be on the other side of the law for once."

Rose sat in a daze. She studied each officer as they stood in front of the room. She couldn't stop the unpleasant feeling coming over her. She shook her head. The Boston Police Commissioner finished making his speech and presentations.

"Our final award will be presented by Captain Morton Dunn of the Boston, Mass. Police Department." Captain Dunn took his place behind the podium. He laid his paper on the stand and began to speak.

Rose stared in shock to see him again. He smiled at her while reading his speech.

"I cannot tell you how proud I am of this next recipient, Rose Hill. I've had the pleasure of meeting her and her grandmother a long time ago in another life. Her courage and dedication are only a few of the attributes she possesses. Bea looked at Rose. She tried getting her attention to no avail.

"Rose? Rose? Bea grew angry. "Isn't that the cop that threw you in jail and caused Jessie's death? Tell me that is not him?"

Rose stood up, still in a daze. She walked past the Mayor, the Commissioner, and all the other officers on the platform.

Bea called out to her, "Rose! Rose! He hasn't called you up yet!"

Rose walked in a daze. The only thing she felt was the anger that had consumed her mind.

Vince called out, "Rose! What are you doing?!"

Rose walked to the edge of the platform, where one of the officers stood. She grabbed his revolver from the holster. The officer whipped around to grab her arm. Rose fought and broke away.

"Don't come near me!" She screamed. I'm going to kill him dead just like he killed my grandmother!"

"Hold your fire!" Morton screamed.

Rose pointed the revolver at Morton crying. "You killed her, now you're going to die!"

Bea called out again. "Rose! Rose!"

The applause rang high. Rose snapped out of her trance. She slowly rose out of her chair and began to walk up to the podium. She walked past the Mayor and then past the Commissioner. She noticed all the other officers. Everyone stood applauding. Rose walked up to the podium and stood next to Morton. He hugged her, then whispered. "I'm sorry, Rose. Please forgive me."

Bea held her breath out of fear of not knowing what Rose would do. Rose looked at Bea for help. Bea mouthed the words "second chance." Rose looked around the room. Mrs. Wilson was there with her daughter and grandchildren. She smiled. Morton looked at her waiting for what to him took forever to come; to be face to face with her again. He wanted her to curse him, kick him, anything, as long as she forgave him. That was the one thing he needed, and only Rose could give it. She smiled again. The anger melted. She whispered, "I forgive you, M.D., I mean Captain Dunn."

"Thank You, Rose." The audience could not hear the words that were spoken but, seeing Rose's smile said enough for Bea. She let out a sigh of relief.

"Speech!" Violet yelled out.

Rose turned to the mic. "I'm not big on public speaking but, I can tell you if I had to do what I did all over again, I would. One of God's commandments: St John 13:34: is to love one another, as I have loved you. Mrs. Wilson needed my help. I was glad to be of service to her. Not because I was so brave like Captain Dunn said but, because it was my reasonable service."

Morton took the mic again. "On behalf of the First National Loan and Finance Company, and the Boston, Massachusetts Police Department, for a job well done, I award you Miss Rose Hill a check for $50,000."

Rose held the check up for all to see. Bea clapped wildly. Rose walked off the platform. She turned and looked at Morton once again. He smiled, "You deserve it."

Rose walked back to her seat. Bea was in tears. Ms. Weathersby gave Rose a hug. "I knew you were special Rose the first day I met you."

Vince took her from Ms. Weathersby's arms.

"What did I tell you, Rose? I'm not the only one who thought you were special. It seems the whole town thinks you are. But none of them love you more than I." They kissed.

Morton walked over, clearing his throat. "Sorry to interrupt Rose but, there was something I wanted to give you before you left."

Vince excused himself. "I'll get the car, Rose."

"Okay, Vince." Rose turned to see what Morton had to show her. He handed her a booklet.

"What's this?"

Morton waited before he answered.

Rose stared at the booklet. She looked up to find Bea. Bea walked over to see what was wrong.

Rose showed her the booklet. They both looked at Morton.

Bea asked first. "Where did you get this?"

Rose continued to stare at the booklet. Morton answered.

"It was all I could do for Jessie. I know it doesn't excuse the hurt I caused you Rose but, it was the least I could do." Morton waited for Rose to say something.

Bea looked at Morton again then spoke herself. "Captain Dunn, I never knew you like Rose and my mother Jessie had in the past, and I must say when I found out who you were and what really happened, I became angry."

Surprised, Morton asked, "your mother, Jessie? "I didn't know Jessie had a daughter living."

"No one did. It was a well-kept secret," said Bea.

"Then you must be Rose's mother. How did you find each other?"

"It's a long story in which I don't care to discuss but, I do want to personally thank you for seeing to it that my mother was put away nicely and not just buried in some unmarked pauper's grave."

Rose stopped staring at her grandmother's picture on the obituary. "So, it was you who paid for everything?"

"Yes Rose, I hoped you didn't mind," Morton spoke, feeling ashamed looking at the floor. "I arranged it so you could attend. Since it was my fault, you were there in the first place. I didn't understand why you didn't come. I know you had your reasons."

Rose turned to Bea. "Ma, I'd like to visit Grandma Jessie's grave. I know she's gone but, I just need to see where she's buried.

"Sure, Rose, we will."

Morton perked up. "I can take you there if you want."

Rose became a bit irritated. "No thanks, Captain Dunn you've done enough already."

Rose turned to walk away but stopped abruptly. "Morton, I mean Captain Dunn, you'll have to excuse me. This forgiveness stuff is still new to me. I meant what I said. I do forgive you but, it's hard not letting the memories of what happened to me and my Grandmother Jessie get in the way."

"I understand Rose, no explanation is necessary."

Bea and Rose both left to get in the Van.

Candy and Stacey jumped in the van first. Candy yelled out the window. "Lunch is on you right, Rose?"

Rose chuckled. "Sure, if they can cash a 50,000.00 check."

"We are not eating out," said Ms. Weathersby. "There is plenty of food left over from dinner last night."

Candy interrupted, "we always eat in! Why can't we eat out sometimes?"

"Leftovers are fine with me. Vince cooks too good to eat out if you ask me," said Bea."

Well, that's fine for you, Ms. Bea but, I've been eating Vince's cooking all my life. I'm not saying it's not good. I just wanted a change."

"You just want to look at boys, and you know it." Violet laughed.

Ms. Clara asked without hesitation. "Rose dear, what are you going to do with your money? Remember, you owe forty dollars for broken dishes?"

"Clara! I swear a six-year-old has better manners," said Ms. Weathersby shaking her head.

Ms. Clara stepped in the van. "Well, I am the treasurer for Farmington House. I was just reminding Rose. I figured with all the excitement she may have forgotten."

Rose laughed. "I remember Ms. Clara."

Chapter 36

Morton left the Civic Center feeling pretty good about himself. Rose has forgiven me, was all he could think about. He didn't mind his thoughts this time, it felt good. He said goodbye to several officers he passed on the way to his car.

Officer Jones called to him, Hey Captain, are you going back to the station?"

"No, Sir, I'm taking the rest of the day off," he said happily.

Officer Jones waved and sped off.

Morton unlocked his car and to his surprise found himself whistling. He hadn't felt that good in a long time, he thought. He started his car and began whistling again. Morton stopped by the grocers to pick up some fruit, sandwich fixings and a bottle of domestic wine. On the elevator ride up he thought of Marla. "Marla, I forgot all about her. I owe her an explanation and an apology. I'll stop by on my way in." As he approached his door, he noticed a note hanging from the doorknob. "Who's selling something now?" He fumbled for his keys to open the door. He pulled the note off the door still fumbling to get the door open. He placed the bags on the floor and began to read the note.

Dear Morton,

I said I wouldn't bother you again. I'm leaving Boston for good. There is no reason for me to stay. I really needed you last night and your pushing me away, only confirmed you didn't need me. My plane leaves in an hour. The time is now 2:15. If you want to give me a reason not to leave, then be at the airport before my plane departs. If I don't see you, I'm gone forever. I realize chances are, you may not get this note in time. Well, I believe in fate and, if it is meant for us to be together, you will find this note in time and stop me from leaving.

I Love You,

Marla

Morton hit the door with his fist. "Aw for Christ Sake! That woman is impossible!"

He quickly opened the door and put his bags on the counter. He checked his watch for the time. "It's 2:30, I'll never make it to the airport in time. It would serve her right if I just leave her there."

Morton changed his uniform, grabbed his keys, and rushed out the door. He looked at his watch again and started talking to himself. "The airport is 20 minutes from here. She would do this today. I was feeling pretty good. I can't believe I'm doing this." He placed the siren on top of his car and took off down the road. He thought to himself, "why is traffic so heavy at this time of day?" He zigzagged in and out of traffic. The traffic going into the airport was moving at a slow and steady pace. He noticed the time on the dashboard. "It's 3:00, in fifteen minutes she'll be gone. Please, God, I'm trying, don't let her leave." Morton parked his car in the emergency vehicle parking area. He ran to the nearest arrival and departure monitor. Frustrated, he searched for the note. "How can I stop her from leaving when I don't know where she is going." He looked at his watch again. "I've got to stop her from leaving."

Over the loudspeaker, he heard the announcement. "Delta Airline flight 289 departing for California is now boarding."

"California! That has to be where she's going!" Morton took off running towards the Delta

Airline terminal. He bumped into a couple of tourists and knocking them over.

"Sorry! Police emergency! An airport security guard saw the commotion. He radioed ahead.

"Zeke! Come in!"

"Yeah, Carl!"

"Zeke, there's a guy running towards you with a gun! Stop Him!"

"A gun? You sure?"

"Zeke, I know a gun when I see one! He almost lost it when he tripped!"

"Alright! Alright! I'll call for backup! You keep up with him!"

Marla stood at the very end of the line inching up closer and closer to the check-in counter.

She looked around several times for Morton. The little hope she had that he may show before her plane left was now growing dim. She sighed and moved up closer, pushing her suitcases with her feet.

Airport security zeroed in on Morton. He slowed his run to a fast pace checking the flight numbers as he went by. He noticed the security guards surrounding him and drawing their weapons.

One of the officers yelled. "Freeze! Don't move! Hands in the air! On the floor now!"

Morton stood still with his hands in the air. Reaching for his badge, he yelled. "I'm a cop!"

"Keep your hands up! Get on the floor!"

Morton fell to the floor. The security men grabbed him and handcuffed his hands around his back.

"I'm a cop, I said. My badge is in my pocket!

I was trying to stop someone from getting on a flight to California! Thanks to you she's probably gone now!"

As Morton was speaking one of the security men checked him for his badge.

"It's here Zeke, said the officer, holding up Morton's badge.

Officer Zeke apologized. "Sorry Captain Dunn, when we saw you running with a weapon well, you can understand how we assumed the worst."

Morton stood dusting himself off. "I can't believe this." He looked at the time. His watch was broken. "Does anybody know what the time is?!"

"It's 3:20 Sir."

Morton walked up closer to the gate. "I'm too late!" He watched the 289 Delta airliner taxi onto the runway. He turned to walk away but tripped over a suitcase and fell.

"Why don't people watch where they put these things?"

Morton stood once again dusting himself off. He looked up, and to his surprise sat Marla, crying with her head down.

"Marla?"

Marla removed her sunglasses, revealing her tears. "Morty? You came!" She jumped around his neck. They both fell to the floor. She kissed him all over his face.

"Marla, let me up, woman! What are you still doing here?!"

Morty helped Marla from the floor.

"I couldn't leave."

Morton trying to stay calm asked, "What do you mean you couldn't leave? I've been through hell trying to get to you before your flight left. I've never had to go through so much for a woman in my life."

Marla took a tissue from her purse and wiped her eyes. "I'm sorry you went through so much trouble, but I'm happy you did. It means you care."

Morton took her by the arm and sat her down. "Now listen Marla, I'm sorry about last night. I promise it won't happen again. I do care about you, and I'd like to get to know you better. We're going to take this thing slow and see where it leads, okay?"

Marla blew her nose in the tissue, nodding in agreement.

"One more thing, no more funny business. I'm too old for this much drama."

"I promise," she said, smiling.

Morton lifted her bags. "Your bags sure are light. What's in them?"

"Nothing," said Marla grinning.

Morton looked inside the suitcases to see if it were true. He shook his head in disgust.

"Unbelievable," was all he could say.

Marla grabbed Morton's arm and walked proudly alongside him, smiling.

About the Author

Julie Pickens was born and raised in Chicago, Illinois. She currently resides in Indianapolis, Indiana with her husband Pastor W.V. Pickens 111 and son Julian G. Pickens. Her love of writing started years ago as a child writing poetry. She plans to continue writing stories for children which she has already begun. She not only has a love for writing but also for singing. Julie wears many hats as First Lady of The Greater Mt Calvary Church. She's the president of GMCMBC Choir, President of the Minister and Deacons wives and widow's ministry. She's a teacher, advisor, decorator and a cook when the need arises. Her favorite scripture is Matt 5:8 Blessed are the pure in heart for they shall see God.

You can contact her at foxthang7@aol.com

The birthing of this book was assisted by:

The Literary Midwife

Helping you get your book from your heart to your reader's hands.
www.hagarfoh.org/literary-midwife

68019057R00115

Made in the USA
Columbia, SC
06 August 2019